Decolonization

Unsung Heroes of the Resistance

Pierre Singaravélou, Karim Miské, and Marc Ball

TRANSLATED FROM THE FRENCH BY WILLARD WOOD

Other Press
New York

Copyright © Arte Éditions/Éditions du Seuil, Paris, 2020
Originally published in French as *Décolonisations* in 2020
by Arte Éditions and Éditions du Seuil, Paris.
English translation copyright © Willard Wood, 2022

Production editor: Yvonne E. Cárdenas
Text designer: Julie Fry
This book was set in Prensa and Franklin Gothic.

1st Printing

Library of Congress Cataloging-in-Publication Data
Names: Singaravélou, Pierre, author. | Miské, Karim, author. |
    Ball, Marc, author.
Title: Decolonization : unsung heroes of the resistance / Pierre
    Singaravélou, Karim Miské, Marc Ball ; translated from the French
    by Willard Wood.
Other titles: Décolonisations. English
Description: New York : Other Press, 2022. | Originally published
    in French as Décolonisations in 2020 by Arte Éditions and Éditions
    du Seuil. | Includes bibliographical references.
Identifiers: LCCN 2022010801 (print) | LCCN 2022010802 (ebook) |
    ISBN 9781635421033 (paperback) | ISBN 9781635421040 (ebook)
Subjects: LCSH: Decolonization — History. | Anti-imperialist
    movements — History.
Classification: LCC JV151 .S4913 2022 (print) | LCC JV151 (ebook) |
    DDC 325/.3 — dc23/eng/20220725
LC record available at https://lccn.loc.gov/2022010801
LC ebook record available at https://lccn.loc.gov/2022010802

Contents

3. The World Is Ours (1956–present)

Preface

DECOLONIZATION. Even the word is deceptive. As if the Western powers suddenly decided to give back control to the people they had conquered. As if, after engaging in such a radical form of domination, it was even possible to return to some hypothetical state of original purity. As if the historical process of decolonization wasn't the upshot of constant rebellions lasting more than a century and extending from India to Senegal, from Algeria to Vietnam, from Kenya to the Democratic Republic of the Congo. As if the engine of change had not been insubordination, rebellion, and insurrection. Countless words and actions that in the end forced white men and women to go home.

So it's time to tell the story the right way around. From the point of view of its main actors: the people seeking their freedom. Give voice to the revolt, this breath of rebellion gusting far and wide. This fierce energy constantly dissipating and regrouping. This phoenix that died in one place only to be reborn in another. This iron will that took shape in the minds of women, the hearts of men, when injustice, wrongfulness, and domination became more unbearable than death itself. When human dignity was trampled underfoot morning, noon, and night. When the invaders from abroad finally got through to the colonized that there would never be equality between them.

When there was nothing left to lose.

It's time to capture this spark, this breath of air, with words and sentences. Harness the poor means available to say the unsayable. This mix of love and hate. This cold rage, dull pain, infinite patience. Putting history back the right way around is like knocking over the table. An accident, a hole in the frame of language. It can't be done with the usual words, with conventional turns of phrase. It calls for rhythm, nerve, transgression. It calls for speaking with the breath of the revolt itself. Breathing with the actors in this story. Accepting that they are the ancestors of us all. Wherever we're from, whatever our skin color, our beliefs, our given name. Because in the end they fought for us all. So that the world might be more habitable for each of us. By taking back control of their own life, the insurgents also freed their oppressors. ■

"Brushing History Against the Grain"

Christopher Columbus, Vasco da Gama, Captain James Cook...Joseph Dupleix, Cecil Rhodes, Charles Gordon, Hubert Lyautey...or yet again Franklin D. Roosevelt, Clement Attlee, Pierre Mendès France, Charles de Gaulle—any well-versed high school student can reel off a list of the heroes of exploration, colonization, and even decolonization. But all of them are of European descent. As though the parties most deeply implicated—the Amerindian, Asian, and African populations—had no part to play. As though, in the role of passive victims or powerless barbarians, they were absent from their own history. This imperial fiction has been debunked by several generations of researchers who have made it their task to restore alternate points of view and to supply the missing parts of a common history. The present book initiates us into this reversal of perspective by focusing on resistance movements against Western colonial domination. It summons up a more complex past than is retailed either by the neocolonialist historians of the former imperial powers or the nationalist historians of the former colonies. Although they privilege opposing political options, both groups overestimate the Europeans' ability to dominate. The supposed omnipotence of the West was a notion welcomed by both the self-satisfied Western elites and the new rulers of the former colonies, who found it a useful political argument both to excuse their derelictions and to maintain their power. The colonial enterprise provoked fierce resistance from the outset in Asia and Africa. The conquest and occasional acquisition of territories was usually a slow process—difficult and never entirely successful. Far from resembling the glossy image of imperial peace, European domination was constantly challenged by activist minorities while a small fraction of indigenous elites cooperated with the colonizers to secure their own social and economic power. This collaboration was a sine qua non of colonial expansion. "To brush history against the grain," Walter Benjamin's felicitous phrase, consists in discovering—from below—the capacity for action of the "colonized," the anonymous women and men who decolonized the contemporary world. And putting back on the shelf once and for all the reassuring hagiographies and imposing nationalist icons, to heed instead the point of the proverb so dear to the Nigerian writer Chinua Achebe: "Until the lions have their own historians, the history of the hunt will always glorify the hunter!"

1. Apprenticeship
(1857–1926)

The Heroic Princess

Lakshmibai, the Rani of Jhansi, a leading figure of the Indian Rebellion of 1857

When does the struggle start? What kicks it off? Where does the spark come from that ignites a revolt? It takes guts to stand up to these white men, with their guns that spray five hundred rounds a minute.

At first, the colonized have no choice. They knuckle under so as not to die like the others. All the sisters, the brothers, the friends who didn't catch on quick enough, who didn't realize there was no resisting. The colonized wait and watch these strange people who think that possessing a powerful technology puts right on their side. They study them and keep the struggle going, but in a different way. The suffering hasn't stopped, but something is also being learned. Eventually, it's time to stand up, to look the colonizer in the eye. Whatever the cost. Time to send him packing, because the awe he once inspired is gone. And on that day it becomes clear that the seeds of the uprising were planted at the outset. Decolonization started on the very first day of colonization.

Where does the struggle start? In whose breast does the rebel yell first form? In the breast of Amankwatia, who was the commander in chief of the Ashanti kingdom that fiercely opposed the British in 1874? Or in the sultan of Aceh's breast, setting off his forty-year war against the Dutch? Or in Lalla Fatma N'Soumer's breast, the mystic female chieftain who led the united tribes of Kabylia against the French in 1854? All of these struggles took place. All of them failed. All of them planted a seed for the future. But none of them echoed as widely as the rebellion that started in India in 1857. It was a total war, upending a whole subcontinent. The British called it the Sepoy Mutiny, but the Indians know it as the First War of Independence. And it was a woman who led this titanic struggle. Her name was Manikarnika Tambe, queen of Jhansi.

Kangana Rahaut, a Bollywood star and supporter of India's ultranationalist prime minister Narendra Modi, played the part of Manikarnika Tambe in the major motion picture *Manikarnika: The Queen of Jhansi*, directed by Radha Krishna Jagarlamudi (2019).

THE INDIA into which Manikarnika Tambe was born in 1828 was rich. Very rich. Its silks, its cotton goods, its delicious spices were exported even to distant Europe by the largest corporation in the world, the British East India Company. From the company's start in 1600 until the middle of the eighteenth century, all went well. Everyone was getting richer, Indians and Englishmen alike. The chartered companies were commercial organizations that enjoyed privileges (monopolies over branches of commerce, diplomatic and legislative authority) granted by the state, through a royal charter. They rapidly became the most efficient instrument of imperial expansion. The East India Company interceded in quarrels between one princely state and another. It helped some states and betrayed others. It recruited an army. Two centuries after its arrival, the company was in control of the entire subcontinent. But it had overlooked one detail. Of its 250,000 soldiers, fully

200,000 were Indians. They were known as sepoys, and their loyalty was anything but guaranteed.

Manikarnika Tambe was from a wealthy high-caste family and received an unusual education for a girl of her circumstances. She not only learned to read, write, and recite poems but was trained in arms and horsemanship. At fourteen she married the maharajah of Jhansi. When he died eleven years later, she succeeded him to the throne, becoming known as the queen of Jhansi. But she wouldn't keep her title for long. The East India Company was gobbling up kingdoms and principalities from one end of the subcontinent to the other. There was no reason for the little state of Jhansi to escape the common fate. Four months into her reign, the queen was pushed aside and her kingdom summarily annexed. The Indians saw these annexations as a series of betrayals. Anger mounted in the countryside, in the cities, among aristocrats and peasants. The sepoys themselves started to voice their objections. Revolt broke out in May 1857. Regiment after regiment rebelled, pooling their forces to fight for India's freedom. When the mutineers reached Jhansi, they massacred the entire British garrison, the soldiers and their families alike. Manikarnika's hour had come.

The queen of Jhansi returned to her throne, created a battalion of women combatants, and organized the resistance. When the British general, Hugh Rose, arrived with his five thousand soldiers to recapture Jhansi, the inhabitants refused to surrender.

Ten days of bombardment followed, and on April 2, 1858, General Rose's cannons breached the walls of the fortress. For the next twenty-four hours there was hand-to-hand fighting in the streets. The British soldiers showed no mercy. Three thousand men, women, and children were indiscriminately killed. The palace was sacked, but Manikarnika managed to escape on horseback.

In 1857 the British army massacred over two thousand sepoys in the fortified palace of Sikandar Bagh in Lucknow. The British photographer Felice Beato, visiting in the spring of 1858, took this photograph of its courtyard.

She joined up, sixty miles away, with the last Indian princes still in active rebellion against the East Indian Company. Riding at their head, the queen of Jhansi led the soldiers for one last attack. The British outnumbered them overwhelmingly. She died fighting, never thinking that she would become the great heroine of Indian independence.

The East India Company did not survive her for long. A month and a half after the last battle, the British parliament dissolved the company for its earlier negligence. The Crown took direct control of India. It was the start of a second and more "modern" form of colonization.

But a new generation of Indians would take up the struggle, inspired by Manikarnika and her companions. They would use new and innovative methods. They only stopped long enough to bandage their wounds. ■

Was India Really Colonized?

The question might seem provocative, given the countless devastating acts of violence perpetrated by the British in India. And it might seem absurd, given the solid block of color assigned to India in the world maps hanging in most school-rooms, suggesting that Britain's hold over the entire subcontinent was uniform, continuous, and total. This familiar representation ignores a large part of India that escaped British rule—namely, the 562 princely states that made up 40 percent of India's land area and supported 25 percent of its population. The princely states were certainly protectorates, and their foreign policy was determined by the colonial authorities, who even intervened at times in the states' domestic affairs. The British meant to exercise indirect rule over these native states, and the states in turn formally recognized British dominion. Yet this indirect rule often masked the actual power relations between Indian sovereigns and Britain's representatives, who usually had to negotiate a compromise. The internal organization of these kingdoms, particularly as it regarded commerce and the law, lay entirely in the hands of the local ruler and, to a lesser extent, the major Indian landowners. Some conservative and authoritarian states—Rajasthan was one—resisted the penetration of foreign cultural influences. Thus Jai Singh, the maharajah of Alwar, based his populist appeal on an ideology of pan-Indian nationalism, supporting the spread of the Hindi language and Hinduism. Other princely states were able to adopt models of "alternative modernity." In the Bhopal district in the late nineteenth century, Queen Shahjahan drew on an egalitarian tradition within Islam, independent of social rank or sex, to promote the rights of women, limit polygamy, and forbid the infanticide of female children. Even in the 60 percent of India under the direct rule of Britain, the sparseness of the colonial administration sometimes allowed local forms of political organization and social regulation to subsist—notably in the realms of law and education, with the persistence of Islamic madrasahs and Hindu schools. The Indian subcontinent thereby partly escaped the colonizers' control.

The Heist of the Century

Makoko, the King of Bateke

In the late nineteenth century, Indigenous people around the world saw defeat in every direction. Westerners were stringing together victories from Cochinchina to Kabylia, plucking sultanates in Borneo like ripe fruit, crushing ex-slaves' rebellions in Jamaica, and shipping back from New Caledonia to the Anthropological Society in Paris the skull of Atai, the last Kanak rebel chief.

Iloo I was king of the Bateke, their makoko, and one of the most powerful men in central Africa. But reports were coming in that two white men, two *mindeles*, were approaching with their weapons, their columns of porters, and their treaty papers to be signed. From the mouth of the river to Lake Malebo, chiefs were signing the treaty, and they weren't asking Iloo for his consent. This was a grave insult, but what recourse did he have? The *mindeles* were dangerous. Iloo hadn't forgotten about Nvita a Kanga, king of the neighboring Bakokos, who had started a war with the Portuguese and ended with his head on a pike.

THE MAKOKO in fact owes his kingdom's wealth to the Portuguese and their slave trade. His ancestors sold slaves to the Portuguese, who piled the slaves into the holds of their ships to work the sugarcane plantations in Brazil. The slave trade enriched the Bateke aristocracy as much as it impoverished the neighboring peoples.

When the British abolished slavery in the 1830s and the French followed suit in the 1840s, the transatlantic slave trade cooled, and the Bateke turned to the sale of ivory. Tons and tons of ivory. The whites paid cash and were always ready to buy more. By 1880 the king of the Bateke was as rich as his father, as rich as his grandfather. But he was uneasy. He learned, in his kingdom on Lake Malebo, that whites were approaching from the north and from the south, armed with new weapons. Making threats and

Among the Bateke, in Congo, the makoko wields secular power while also mediating between the living and their ancestors, between men and spirits. He embodies both the spiritual and temporal power of the ancestors.

offering rich presents, they were bringing the Bateke chiefs over to their side. The strategy was working so well that some of the chiefs were now openly defying the makoko. To foil the plotters, the Bateke king would enter into an alliance with Pierre Savorgnan de Brazza, the first white man to reach him. Brazza, an aristocrat with a taste for glory and adventure, was intent on carving out an empire for France in central Africa.

The makoko organized a big ceremony in Brazza's honor. The explorer had applied to open a trading post on Lake Malebo, and the request was hard to refuse as Brazza made it clear that there would be war unless Iloo signed. With great pomp, and in the presence of his subjects and the high priest, the makoko signed

this treaty preserving his power — little realizing that he had signed over to the French his hereditary rights to the land.

Brazza had stolen a march on his great rival, the Welsh explorer Henry Morton Stanley. For two years, Stanley had been crisscrossing the region as an agent of Leopold II of Belgium. Like the French, Leopold wanted to create an empire in the heart of Africa. In pursuit of his patron's ambitious dream, Stanley had navigated rapids, hacked through forests, and pierced mountains, blasting a passage with dynamite. He was known locally as Boula Matari, the rock breaker. Thanks to his superior weaponry, he had also broken the resistance of the tribes that tried to stop his advance. When he finally reached Lake Malebo, which he renamed Stanley Pool, he drew up the boundaries of the Belgian king's future state. But Stanley was furious to discover that Brazza's treaty with the

At the center of the photograph stands Henry Morton Stanley (just left of the ladder), the famous British explorer chosen by King Leopold II to create a colony in Congo.

makoko gave France the lake's northern shore and part of the Congo River — territories that would slip from Leopold's grasp.

The race between France and King Leopold heightened military tensions in the region. The Portuguese, backed by the British, reacted by threatening to shut off access to the mouth of the Congo River. The controversy seemed on track to start a European war, something that Germany, with its interests in southwest Africa, wanted to avoid at all costs. To resolve the Congo question and at the same stroke settle all the other contentious issues between European nations on the African continent, Chancellor Bismarck organized a conference in Berlin.

The conference was a success. On February 26, 1885, the European powers signed an agreement that created an "independent" state of Congo as the private property of King Leopold. And France, Britain, Germany, Portugal, Spain, and Italy would divide the rest of the continent among them, setting the foundation for a new era of European colonialism. ■

Berlin 1885, the Internationalization of European Imperialism

Not a single African. When diplomats from fourteen countries gathered at the great conference in Berlin from November 15, 1884, to February 26, 1885, not a single African was among them. Partitioning the continent was not officially discussed. After a century of European exploration, the issue at hand was to promote free trade and movement across the basins of the Congo and Niger Rivers. The old and new colonizers decided to reach an agreement now so as to avoid later confrontations that might lead to war. Whenever a new territory was acquired, the other colonial powers were to be notified. What crystallized at the Berlin conference was the realization among European nations of a shared expansionist imperative, operating within an accepted framework of regulations. The tangible upshot of this collective colonialism was a commission to ensure the neutrality of the Congo Basin and a plan proposed by King Leopold of Belgium for an international colony in the same region. This wave of European colonialism adopted a humanitarian guise: the signatories undertook to improve "the moral and material conditions of existence" of the native populations and to take part in efforts to end the slave trade and slavery. At the same time, each nation was covertly trying to define and consolidate its sphere of influence. And the agreements signed in the final stages of the conference were quickly undermined: the international commission was never created; the Congo Free State, the personal property of King Leopold, kept all its ivory and rubber for its own concessionary companies. Although competition and protectionism seem to have been the order of the day, the colonial powers took care to cooperate among themselves to preserve and extend their trading privileges and territorial conquests across the globe.

Filling Skulls

From a British phrenology magazine, 1890s

By partitioning Africa at the Berlin conference, the European powers inherited a continent and its vast resources. But also its inhabitants. One hundred million colonial subjects lived under their administration. Treating them as equals was out of the question, it defeated the whole purpose of colonization. So what was to be done with them? Europeans are a civilized people. After all, they invented human rights and did away with slavery. They needed justification for their domination of the conquered peoples of Africa and Asia. Fortunately, scientists were able to provide what they needed. For several decades already, they had been working at dissecting and classifying humans.

AT THE PRESTIGIOUS Société d'Anthropologie de Paris, the question that currently preoccupied the doctors, zoologists, and famous scientists was the superiority of the white race. No technique that might possibly lead to an answer was being overlooked. And craniometry was drawing much attention. Researchers were busily measuring the size, volume, facial angle, and cephalic index of all the skulls that had been brought back from the colonies.

Until one day, a troublemaker appeared on the scene, a Black man, a person whose skull size would normally have been the subject of measurement, except that he was a member of the anthropological society. To the Parisian elite of the day, Anténor Firmin was not really a Black like the rest of them. A newspaper editor and politician, he belonged to the ruling class of Haiti, a country that had been brought into being by a slave rebellion in the early nineteenth century, the first Black republic in modern history. In Paris, Haitians were perceived as being more civilized than Africans, and this prejudice allowed Firmin to be admitted to the anthropological society. His white colleagues saw him as the exception that confirms the rule.

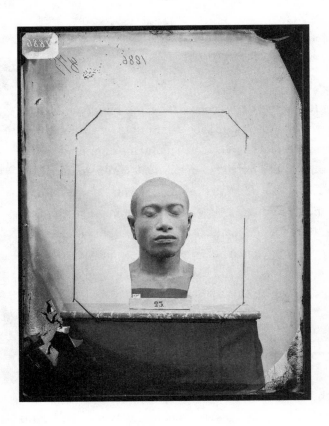

Not for a minute did they suspect that Anténor Firmin was on a mission, that even before leaving Haiti he'd set himself the goal of using science to disprove the idea of white supremacy. The year was 1885, the same year that Africa was divided up, the same year that the French premier, Jules Ferry, calmly told the Chamber of Deputies that the "superior races" had a duty to civilize the "inferior races." In the white world, this struck everyone as normal, obvious, and unobjectionable. Firmin knew he had to avoid even the slightest error. To add to the challenge, he'd decided to refute the theories of Paul Broca, the founder of the Société d'Anthropologie de Paris. Broca was the tutelary figure among French anthropologists and had died just five years earlier. The society's other members would probably not enjoy seeing their former leader's statue toppled by their new Haitian colleague.

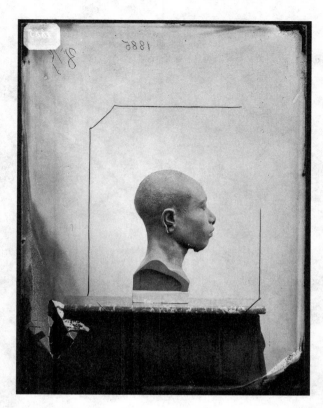

Paul Broca had spent his career filling skulls with lead and comparing the results. His conclusion was plain: the white race was the most intelligent because it had the greatest cranial capacity. Firmin analyzed Broca's numbers. He realized they didn't make sense. He deduced that the French scientist had deliberately altered the results to bolster his model of racial hierarchy. To make his case, the Haitian scientist published his book *Of the Equality of Human Races*, in which he raised the question, How could learned and intelligent men have been so thoroughly blinded by their passions? Firmin attributed his colleagues' blindness to the myths and legends they had absorbed in their youth, myths that convinced them of the superiority of their own civilization and entrenched their belief that slavery and colonialism were legitimate. Somewhat ironically, Firmin hoped that his

In the nineteenth century, scientists such as Paul Broca measured cranial capacity with lead pellets, water, or sand. They held that the volume of a skull was directly correlated to intelligence.

writings, by holding up a mirror to his colleagues, would make them see their error and return to reason. But this was not to be. With their conquest of the world now almost complete, Europeans had no interest in seeing themselves in the unflattering mirror the Haitian scientist held up to them. They far preferred visiting ethnographic exhibitions. There, at least, representations of "inferior races" were kept in their place. ■

The Growth of the "Colonial Sciences"

From the end of the nineteenth century to the successive decolonizations of the 1950s and 1960s, scientists from the colonial powers alongside "native" intellectuals developed new subdisciplines—which gradually gained a permanent place in universities and centers of learning—devoted wholly or in part to "colonial sciences." The body of knowledge brought together under this rubric, most of it deriving from the social sciences, fulfilled an apparently contradictory set of functions. It was meant to legitimize the colonial project by pointing to the rational and "humanitarian" aspects of colonization, which would make every corner of the empire an example of civilization and progress. Until the end of World War II, therefore, the new field of colonial studies often propagandized on behalf of the empire. At the same time, the "colonial sciences" provided a scientific field whose researchers actively participated in the intellectual development of the humanities and social sciences. The incorporation of colonial studies into academia went beyond the creation of specialized courses and professorships. Experts in the field and university affiliates found their way into the network of research institutes, learned societies, museums and expositions, scientific journals, and publishing houses, both specialized and general. These new disciplines contributed to the functioning of colonial administrations and the economic prosperity of the empire by identifying an array of "good" practices. They also fleshed out the education of future colonists and developed models of colonial public policy. The twin functions of these disciplines—epistemological on the one hand and practical on the other, or intellectual and political—help explain the massive involvement of scientists from both sides of the political spectrum, including some European and "native" anticolonialists, in the "work" of the colonial sciences. Scientists and the social sciences were therefore at the heart of the European colonial project, with colonization conceived from the outset as an intellectual enterprise.

Alice in Leopold Land

In October 1888, John Boyd Dunlop was watching his son ride his tricycle with great effort over the uneven cobblestones of their courtyard in Dublin, wishing he could help him. Suddenly he had an idea. If he hollowed out the tire and put an inflatable rubber tube inside, his son's wheels would roll smoothly over the bumpy ground. This was the birth of the inner tube, a revolutionary invention that would change the daily life of Europeans. And create an unprecedented surge in the demand for rubber.

For Belgium's King Leopold II, the rise in the price of natural rubber was an unexpected boon. The state he had recently created in Congo with the help of Henry Morton Stanley, which he ran like a private company, was failing financially. The inexhaustible market for inflatable inner tubes provided him with a ready-made solution. Congo was overrun with vines rich in latex. Leopold had only to exploit the country's forests on a large scale. But harvesting latex is an extremely labor-intensive task, and the Congolese did not turn to it willingly. The population took up arms against the soldiers of the Force Publique, Leopold's militarized police. Five years later, knowing the war to be unwinnable, the local villagers surrendered.

This was the moment chosen by Alice Seeley Harris, an idealistic young Englishwoman, to establish a Protestant mission in the heart of Congo.

My husband and I first came to the Congo in 1898. We were missionaries there for seven years. I initially taught in the school, because our predecessors had gone on vacation. During our stay, our relations with the Belgian rubber producers became very tense.

— ALICE SEELEY HARRIS

INTENT ON SHARING the word of Christ and the benefits of civilization, Alice and John Harris were not prepared for the horrendous conditions they discovered on arrival. King Leopold wanted his territory to generate a profit and had set impossibly high rubber production quotas. The vines quickly became exhausted, and workers had to push deeper into the forest every day to keep their Belgian overseers happy. All available means were used to force the villagers to work in untenable conditions.

> *The rubber vine, which is native to the Congo, should only be tapped twice a year, at most. But the Belgians insisted on tapping it twice a month. The native inhabitants therefore had to go into the forest constantly. If they didn't bring back enough rubber, their wives and children were often taken hostage and jailed until the quota was filled.*
>
> **— ALICE SEELEY HARRIS**

The level of violence kept rising. When beatings failed to produce the desired yields, the native soldiers were ordered to start a large-scale campaign of murder. Terror became a tool of human resource management. Protestant missionaries, who witnessed the brutality firsthand, tried to alert the public to it, but they were unsuccessful. John and Alice Harris had a taste of this when they returned to London for their first vacations and found it almost impossible to convince their friends of the great horror being perpetrated in Congo. So Alice decided to buy herself one of the first commercially available portable cameras, the Kodak Brownie, and she used it to take the snapshot that would change the playing field.

> *One Sunday morning when I was alone, the boy came to tell me that a native man was waiting to see me behind the mission station. He was carrying the severed hand and foot of his young daughter, wrapped in plantain leaves. I had him sit on the steps of the veranda, and he opened*

the plantain leaf with the hand and foot inside. I took their photograph.
The hand and the foot were there, in front of my eyes.

— ALICE SEELEY HARRIS

The girl who'd been killed and dismembered was named Boali. Mutilation was common in Congo at the time, and it was often performed on the living. When the white overseers sent out troops to kill the inhabitants of a village in the crazy hope of making them increase their rubber production, they ordered the soldiers to collect a severed hand from each person killed. But the soldiers, who preferred to save their ammunition for hunting, often just cut off the victim's hand or foot. In return, they were given more ammunition to use on the next mission.

Alice and her missionary colleagues took many pictures of Congolese with mutilations and sent them to Edmund Morel, a British activist working to put a stop to these atrocities. The incontrovertible evidence of the pictures provoked the first humanitarian scandal in modern times. The greedy and blood-thirsty King Leopold II became public enemy number one in England and the United States. To stir up public reaction even more, Morel sent Alice and John Harris off on a speaking tour, equipped with a slide projector. From London to Manchester, and from New York to Minneapolis, audiences in churches and auditoriums were shocked and astonished at the treatment of the Congolese. In Belgium too, public opinion started to change. The ground was shifting under Leopold's feet, and in 1908 he was forced by Parliament to turn over the management of his personal colony in Congo to the Belgian government. Alice Seeley Harris and Edmund Morel won their battle against the Belgian king, but the twentieth century was still only just beginning, and Congolese independence was not even a remote possibility. The reformers' hope was to bring about a more humane form of colonization.

If such a thing exists.

Alice Seeley Harris, a missionary, triggered the first humanitarian scandal of the nineteenth century with her photographs of natives of Belgian Congo whose hands had been cut off.

While the Western newspapers focused on the scandal in Congo, another large-scale crime was quietly being perpetrated nearby in the German colony of German Southwest Africa. Two

ethnic groups, the Herero and the Nama, had had the audacity to start a rebellion against the colonists who were appropriating their land. The German emperor and his representative, General Lothar von Trotha, responded harshly.

On October 2, 1904, von Trotha announced: "Within the German borders every Herero, with or without a gun, with or without

Nsala of Wala looks at the foot and hand of his five-year-old daughter, Boali, killed and dismembered by soldiers of King Leopold's army. The photograph was taken by Alice Seeley Harris at her mission in Ikau, Congo.

cattle, will be shot." In his journal he wrote, "I believe that this nation, as such, should be annihilated."

The survivors were imprisoned in concentration camps, where two scientists with promising futures, Eugen Fischer and Theodor Mollison, performed medical experiments on them. When Fischer and Mollison returned to Germany, they would teach racial anthropology. Their most prominent student, Josef Mengele, would deploy his talents at the Auschwitz death camp from 1943 to 1945. ■

"Every Herero Will Be Shot":
The Forgotten Genocide

Although it remained forgotten until the 1980s, the first genocide of the twentieth century took place in German Southwest Africa over a simple question of land. The Hereros and the Namas—whose lands and cattle were increasingly being taken from them and whom the Germans further angered by constructing a railroad line and confining them to reservations—started a rebellion. In January 1904 they killed a hundred German colonists, sparing the women and children. The German authorities seized on the opportunity to eliminate the two Indigenous groups entirely, denouncing their members as racially inferior and as obstructing German colonists trying to settle the land and exploit its mineral riches. On August 11, 1904, during the battle of Hamakari, General Lothar von Trotha, known as "the Shark," killed five thousand combatants and executed twenty-five thousand civilians. He then ordered the shooting of "every Herero, with or without a gun." The survivors were forced to flee into the Omaheke Desert, where most died of hunger, thirst, or exhaustion. In October the Nama people's rebellion suffered the same fate. Thousands of Hereros and Namas were then placed in concentration camps, where the majority died of disease or exhaustion.

German doctors, directed by Eugen Fischer, conducted medical experiments on the adult prisoners as well as on several hundred of the children. These experiments, which included sterilization and injection with smallpox, typhus, and tuberculosis, took place some forty years before Nazi doctors conducted similar experiments in World War II concentration camps. Hundreds of skulls were sent to Germany. At the end of what von Trotha conceived and carried out as a "racial war," 80 percent of the Herero nation and half of the Nama people had been killed, all in less than four years. In 1985, following a Herero campaign of redress, the United Nations acknowledged the genocidal character of these massacres. In 2004 the German government officially apologized to the Nama and Herero but stopped short of offering any financial reparation. Between 2011 and 2018 at the request of the Republic of Namibia, Herero skeletons still conserved in German universities were restored to their country of origin.

Mohun Bagan's Revenge

Mahatma Gandhi and Sarojini Naidu on the Salt March, 1930

And then one day, the tables start to turn. It's been fifty years since the last battle, the last victorious show of force by the colonizers, the last defeat of the colonized. Fifty years during which the natives have watched their occupiers, scrutinized them. Attended their schools and learned their ideas. Discovered where their power comes from. But challenging the colonizer on the battlefield has high costs. There are other arenas in which to confront them. Arenas that the colonizer himself has defined.

For the British, at the beginning of the twentieth century, sport was a serious business. So serious they'd decided to use it as a civilizing instrument in the colonies. The indolent natives would learn the manly virtues by being taught to play cricket, rugby, and soccer. And at the same time, the colonizer would demonstrate his superiority. But things don't always go as planned...

ON JULY 29, 1911, at teatime, sports enthusiasts from all parts of Bengal make their way to the stadium in Calcutta, the capital of the British Empire in India. The event is such a draw that the railroad company has to schedule extra trains to accommodate all the fans. For the first time in the history of India's soccer championships, a "native" team, Mohun Bagan, has reached the finals. On this evening they are to play the British soldiers of the East Yorkshire Regiment. Tens of thousands of spectators mill around the stadium. Most never manage to get in. The players on the Mohun Bagan team are all Hindus, and normally their fans are too. Muslim soccer fans would typically root for the Mohammedan Sporting Club. But on this night, with Mohun Bagan playing the English, all of Bengal is united, and the spectators count as many Muslims as Hindus.

Satyagraha, or "truth force," was a principle put forward by Mahatma Gandhi in India. It advocated resistance through nonviolence and civil disobedience.

The two main religious groups in Bengali society, which are rallying on this night around Mohun Bagan, also support the nationalist Swadeshi movement, whose guiding idea is simple: boycott British products and buy Indian. The stakes are considerable: India in general and Bengal in particular provide important markets for the goods made in Manchester's mills. Swadeshi activists support Indian industries instead, dealing a blow to the British economy. Indians are taking back control and establishing a boundary. All over Bengal, supporters of the boycott are making a show of resistance, burning British-made clothes on the public square.

But at the heart of the Swadeshi movement, and what makes it so popular, is its cultural resistance. Its reclaiming of Indian heritage. Its ability to take an apparently minor issue and make it a symbol of the wider struggle. Take sports shoes, for instance. Indians, whether Hindu or Muslim, don't wear leather shoes. Religious prohibition plays a part in it, but so does cultural tradition. Even on the soccer field they don't wear shoes. And until Mohun Bagan reached the finals, the fact always amused the English. But tonight they're not laughing as they square off against the eleven intrepid barefoot players who just beat the Rifle Brigade and the First Middlesex Regiment, two well-trained and well-shod British military teams. Not so funny, in fact, to realize that beyond the

This photograph shows British textiles being burned. The Swadeshi (self-rule) movement, launched in 1905 as part of India's push for independence, called for the boycott of British goods.

eleven players on the field and the tens of thousands of supporters around the stadium, all India sides with this team. The war that the sepoys lost in 1858 is being replayed on the lawn of the Calcutta Football Ground.

When, at the end of the regulation ninety minutes, Mohun Bagan wins by a score of two to one, the stadium erupts in cheers! Ecstatic fans rip off their shirts, and members of the Mohammedan Sporting Club celebrate their Hindu brothers' victory by rolling on the ground. The whole Indigenous city rejoices in the victory of the barefoot Bengalis. The following day, July 30, 1911, the Calcutta newspaper *Nayak* sums up the feelings of an entire people: "Every Indian person will be proud and happy to learn that the rice-eating, malaria-infested and barefoot Bengalis have beaten the Herculean beef-eating British at their own game." ■

Sports in the Colonies: Imperialism or Cultural Globalization?

Starting in the mid-nineteenth century, European soldiers, teachers, and missionaries introduced sports originally from Britain into their colonies. Thus, English soldiers spread soccer throughout the Black population of southern Africa, and rugby became popular with the Afrikaner prisoners after the Boer War (1899–1902). The colonizers were convinced that sports were a means of transmitting moral values such as loyalty and the work ethic, attributes that were not only essential to turning out good soldiers but that would provide the natives access to the benefits of civilization. In practice, the sports world was highly segregated. In Algeria, for instance, separate sports clubs were created for each ethnic group. The Muslims, French, Italians, Spanish, and Jews each had their own. Yet although sports could become an expression of cultural imperialism, most sports traditions were adopted voluntarily, and they often underwent a deep transformation at the hands of the colonizers and the colonized, occasionally to the point of becoming a central element of national identity, as cricket has become in India. Its enormous popularity among the Indian nobility owes to its intellectual and strategic elements but also to the fact that it involves no direct contact between opponents, nor any great expenditure of physical energy, features that would have been incompatible with aristocratic dignity. Indigenous peoples adapted sports to their local conditions, as the youth of Congo did in the 1930s, playing soccer in narrow streets or on the edge of roads, replacing the soccer ball with green lemons or balls made of paper or even white latex. In these new conditions, the game's tactics evolved, gradually leaving behind the British kick-and-rush style of long passes for a more individual game emphasizing improvisation and ball control. Yet some Indigenous sports traditions could maintain a challenge to the colonial order. In the working quarters of Bombay, during the years between the two world wars, the *akhada* (gymnasiums) were closely watched by the police as places where politics and labor unions were hotly discussed, and because the young men who gathered there took active part in social movements. Beating the colonists at their own game became a symbolic weapon in the anticolonial struggle. For instance, the soccer team representing Algeria's National Liberation Front (Front de libération nationale, FLN) went on several international tours during the 1950s to publicize the cause of Algerian independence.

World War I: The Black Force

Senegalese soldiers of the 43rd Battalion who fought
in the recapture of Fort Douaumont, 1916

Among the colonists, there was a general feeling of gloom. Anxiety too. Mohun Bagan's victory might seem a small thing, but it wasn't. It signaled a crack in the armored surface of the British Empire. A foretaste of a possible rebellion. But right now, tensions were rising in Europe, and that's what preoccupied the British. Three years after Mohun Bagan's historic victory, World War I broke out. Britain joined with France and Russia to confront Germany, Austro-Hungary, and the Ottoman Empire. If Britain was to have any chance of victory, it needed troops, more troops, and still more troops. A million Indian soldiers took ship for Europe, the Middle East, and East Africa. The war was being fought on every front.

FRANCE, which controlled the second largest empire after Britain, would also summon hundreds of thousands of soldiers from its colonies. Never had so many Algerians, Indochinese, and Senegalese disembarked at the port of Marseilles. Never had so many subjects from the colonies set foot on French soil. The experience would change these men forever.

When the soldier Lamine Senghor arrived in the south of France from Senegal in early 1916, the war had reached a stalling point, and no end was in sight. For him, as for his comrades, France meant the military base at Fréjus where he had to rehearse the same maneuvers day after day and listen to the same orders. But unlike most of his comrades, Senghor knew the French well. In Dakar, he had worked for Maurel et Prom, the biggest peanut exporter in Senegal. The French army officers reminded him of the company foremen who'd taken pleasure in demeaning him. But now he was in France, Lamine Senghor didn't expect his officers to talk to him in pidgin, implying that Blacks would never

These Senegalese tirailleurs came from every part of West Africa to serve in the French colonial forces. More than 160,000 Africans and Madagascans were recruited for World War I. Tens of thousands lost their lives in the conflict.

understand proper French. As he came to realize, Blacks weren't really being asked to understand. They were there because of their physical strength, their bravery.

After the war, which he survived, and once he'd embarked on his career as a political activist, Senghor started to understand the reason he and his comrades had been brought to France. He would learn about *The Black Force*, a book written in 1910 by General Charles Mangin, which prescribed the massive use of African soldiers in the event of a European war. He would learn that also in 1910, Adolphe Messimy, later to be the Minister of the Colonies, wrote these words in an influential French newspaper: "Africa cost us mountains of gold, thousands of soldiers, and rivers of blood; we do not expect to get our gold back, but the men and blood must be repaid to us with interest."

For the moment, though, Lamine Senghor knew nothing of all this. Sent forth from the base at Fréjus, he found himself suddenly at the front. In hell.

Shells screamed overhead, the noncoms barked out orders, the wounded cried out for help. Mud, rain, and fog. With a bayonetted rifle and sixty-five pounds of equipment on his back, Senghor went on the attack.

Concentrate on making it through.

He fell and got up. He dodged bullets, he cheated death. The object was to come back in one piece. He thought of his mother, his brothers, his sisters. He thought of the women of Dakar, their beauty, the bewitching smell of incense that perfumed their kikois.

By January 1917, two and a half years into the war, the morale of the French troops was at low ebb. General Nivelle, commander in chief of the armies, instructed his subordinates to "not spare black blood, if it will save some white." Three months later, on orders from General Mangin, the proponent of "black force,"

Senegalese and Indochinese tirailleurs parade through the streets of Paris on July 14, 1913.

Lamine Senghor was among fifteen thousand colonial infantry-men launched at the ridge of the Chemin des Dames, to their almost certain death. At dawn, with an icy wind blowing, he found the trenches strewn with corpses. His battalion had been destroyed by a mustard gas attack. Senghor survived, but his lungs were badly injured. He was sent back to the rear at Fréjus to recover.

All the wounded soldiers from the colonial empire were gathered in the military hospitals along the Côte d'Azur, and it made Senghor think. Hundreds of thousands of men with dark skins, both black and brown, had been transported across the oceans to die from the bullets of an enemy they didn't know, in a war that didn't concern them. In the camp where he was trying to recover his health and return to life, Lamine Senghor realized the full absurdity of this war of the whites, the *toubabs*. He could see from the way the noncommissioned officers looked at him that, despite his sacrifice, he would always be treated in this country as a native, a second-class citizen.

Their looks defiled him. To purify himself, Lamine Senghor would spend the rest of his life fighting the colonial order. ∎

The Time for Rebellion Is at Hand

With World War I underway, opposition movements and rebellions started to stir in the four corners of Europe's empires. The colonial powers were drawing massively on their far-flung colonies for military recruits, manual laborers, natural resources, and money. The long and costly conflict, whose key players were European, had a profoundly disintegrating effect on Indigenous societies. Close to 190,000 Indigenous people worked in France, particularly in weapons factories.

In the colonies, taxes on rural populations increased enormously—a jump of 30 percent, for instance, in French West Africa. To boost the production of strategic commodities such as castor oil, a lubricant for airplanes and ships, the authorities resorted to forced labor, diverting workers away from producing food. These wartime requisitions caused price hikes and shortages, along with corresponding unrest among colonial subjects—as when Egyptians rose up in reaction to the hardships imposed by the war effort and urged King Fuad to officially request independence from Britain in November 1918. The British mobilized their Indian army for the war effort, a force of 1,400,000 men, while France recruited 580,000 soldiers from its African and Asian colonies. Hundreds of thousands of porters were also drafted, many of whom died of exhaustion, illness, or hunger.

The enlistment of Indigenous peoples had its setbacks. Many men fled into the mountains, jungles, or neighboring colonies in order to escape conscription. The recruitment effort provoked a widespread rebellion in the French colony of Upper Volta, from November 1915 to September 1916. That month, young Algerians in Constantine Province reacted to the forced military recruitment by sabotaging telegraph lines and attacking European residents. These acts quickly escalated into a nationalist insurrection: the Algerian Republic was declared at Boumequeur on November 11, 1916. A brutal suppression followed in 1917: many villages were destroyed, and almost three hundred insurrectionists were executed.

Resistance in India was fomented by the Indian diaspora, which sought to use the global conflict to free the homeland from British occupation. Sikhs who had settled in Canada and California joined to form the Ghadar (Rebellion) Party in San Francisco in 1913 and created cells of partisans on the subcontinent. Their attempt at a general rebellion failed in February 1915. That same year, the first free Indian government would be established in Kabul by Mahendra Prata, with the support of a German government keen to weaken the British Empire, but the plan did not survive the war. These many opposition movements forced the colonial elites to promise reforms that would be favorable to the colonized—promises that were betrayed once the war ended.

A Woman Insurgent

Kikuyu women with gourds they used to carry water

Hundreds of thousands of Indigenous soldiers—from India, North Africa, Indochina, and sub-Saharan Africa—died in order for their French and British masters, and their US allies, to conquer Germany. But the colonial powers had no intention of rewarding this sacrifice by giving the "natives" more freedom.

ON THE HIGH PLATEAUS of Kenya, for example, land was being confiscated on all sides. The British colonial government had instituted a lottery system and was distributing vast amounts of land to English combat veterans. From one day to the next, a Kikuyu farmer whose forebears had lived on the land for centuries might have to give up his farm to a bus driver from Manchester or a cobbler from Liverpool. Furthermore, he would be forced to work for the newcomer — forced labor for which he received a pittance.

But according to Kikuyu cosmogony, it was Ngai, God himself, who had revealed the Kikuyu homeland to Gikuyu, their ancestor, from the summit of Mount Kenya. And it was Ngai who had made Mumbi, Gikuyu's wife, appear under a fig tree.

These were the three pillars of the Kikuyu's existence: God, Land, and Women.

By confiscating their land, therefore, the British had cut the Kikuyus' ties with Ngai. That left them only their women. But why shouldn't the colonists appropriate them too? Forced labor for the women! The colonists' greed knew no bounds.

On the coffee plantations, night after night, the "native" foremen would pick out a victim. Systematic rape. And the British planters turned a blind eye. As long as it didn't reduce yields. The women who got pregnant were sent back to their families, where they often met with rejection.

Kikuyu women in Kenya were forced to work the coffee harvest on British plantations.

To avoid this fate, Mary Muthoni Nyanjiru set out one day for Nairobi, the capital of the colony, the city where anything was possible.

In Nairobi, there was no forced labor. In Nairobi, there was no arranged marriage. In Nairobi, you could decide your own fate. As long as you obeyed the Englishman's law. From the train station, Mary crossed the white city, a section of town the natives might pass through but didn't live in. She saw houseboys, rickshaw coolies, gardeners. After walking for forty-five minutes, Mary reached Pangani, the Black part of town, on the other side of the river. This was where adventurers and drifters ended up, those who, having lost their land and their jobs, went looking for another life. Most of the Kikuyu women in Pangani lived by selling their bodies or brewing beer. Some people looked down on them, but they didn't care. After all, they were richer than the men who bought their favors. These were strong women, solidly planted on their feet, and they accepted Mary as one of them.

British colonial administrators distribute flour to the Kikuyu, who worked as forced laborers.

They were women busily inventing a new society, a society not controlled by men.

Like them, Mary passionately followed the first labor strikes of the Kikuyu women who worked on coffee plantations. Like them, she was incensed when the English outlawed the brewing of traditional beer. Like them, she became a supporter of Harry Thuku, a Christian anticolonial activist who led the struggle to end women's forced labor.

Mary believed in Thuku's cause. It gave her hope. Harry Thuku wore a suit, spoke English, and was not afraid of the colonists. Things were finally going to change for Kikuyu women. When, on March 14, 1922, the colonial authorities arrested Harry Thuku on charges of being a native agitator, Mary's blood came to a boil. With her women friends from Pangani, she joined the demonstration in front of the Nairobi police station. It was the first demonstration ever in the colony's new capital.

Several thousand people congregated peacefully on the public square, sitting, standing, talking, singing, and praying. The atmosphere changed when the organizers announced it was time for everyone to go home. Mary couldn't believe her ears. Harry Thuku was still in prison. There was no question of their leaving without him. As she stood up in front of the leaders of the movement to address them, she made the strongest gesture a Kikuyu woman could make, a gesture that told the men they were unfit for power. Facing the astonished comrades of the imprisoned leader, Mary Nyanjiru lifted her dress and exposed her nudity.

Take my dress and give me your trousers! You men are all cowards! What are you waiting for? Our leader is in this jail! Let's go free him!

— MARY NYANJIRU

The Pangani women gave a great shout and together rushed the police station. Thousands of men followed behind. The government soldiers fired into the crowd. Hit by a bullet, Mary died instantly. Dozens of protesters fell at her side.

Harry Thuku spent nine years in prison, and the British believed they had crushed the rebellion in its infancy. But for decades, at night, when the Kikuyus gathered to talk, they kept alive the memory of Mary Muthoni Nyanjiru, the woman who refused to give up. And when the next generation of rebels came along, it was Mary's name they invoked as they set off for battle. ■

The Women's War

When on November 23, 1929, the colonial authorities in Oloko, Southern Nigeria, were confronted with a mounting political movement against them, they contemptuously called it "rioting," "mutiny," or "unrest." But on the native side, the movement was known, in the Igbo and Ibibio languages, as *Ogu Umunwaye* and *Ekong iban*, meaning the "Women's War." Women sent out a coded call to muster using the leaves of palm-oil trees, and when they demonstrated on December 2 in the village of Oloko before the office of the warrant chief, Okugo, asking for his dismissal and a trial, they numbered more than ten thousand. Within a few weeks, the protest had spread throughout the eastern portion of the country. The women were galvanized by the threat of a tax increase, along with a rise in school costs and the pressure to engage in forced labor.

But the evil the women were responding to went deeper than that. The intrusion of Europeans into Nigeria, with their promotion of patriarchal principles and a misogynistic ideology, had abruptly deprived women of the political and religious power they had traditionally enjoyed. Till then, they had participated in government and held a major role in the local economy and in the long-distance trade: the most successful women gained the prestigious chieftaincy title of *iyalode*. Vernacular legends described periods when women were the actual rulers. When power was put wholly into the hands of Indigenous men, there was corruption and abuse of power.

Under the leadership of three women—Ikonnia, Nwannedia, and Nwugo—who became known as the "Oloko Trio," the women protesters would gather at the house of a presumed wrongdoer to air their complaints with dance and song, mocking the man and his virility. Sometimes they would destroy his hut or cover it in mud. A number of warrant chiefs were forced to quit as a result. In all, the women protesters raided and destroyed several banks, a dozen Indigenous courts, and some storehouses—tools and symbols of colonial oppression. They attacked jails and freed the prisoners. These actions were unacceptable to the British, who responded with bloody reprisals: fifty-five women were executed in Abak from December 14 to 16, 1929. A commission of enquiry gathered testimony from British colonial officials and women activists in March 1930. When this great protest movement came to an end and the dust had settled, women had improved their lot in society and earned the right to serve in the Indigenous courts. Some even became warrant chiefs.

The Pariah's Conscience

Blaise Diagne and the other ministers of Pierre Laval's government, 1932

France recognizes us when she needs our soldiers, but she continues to treat us like lesser creatures when the danger is past.

— LAMINE SENGHOR

PARIS, 1924. Rather than return to Dakar and resume his life as a "native," Lamine Senghor built a life for himself in the empire's capital city. Here he was the white man's equal, at least on paper. As a veteran who'd fought for France in World War I, he was able to get a job in the postal service, in Paris's nineteenth arrondissement. His wife, Eugénie Comont, was as French as they come, and they had two children. It was a working-class life, a man-of-the-people's life, with the difference that his skin was black.

He had come to know Paris's working-class districts, to recognize the anger of its people, which was so close to his own. They talked of exploitation, of the bosses, of the fight against big capital. It all resonated with Senghor, who added to the litany a few words of his own: colonialists, racism, forced labor. The fire of rebellion roared in his lungs, which had been almost destroyed by the brutal war. Recently, he'd been writing for *Le Paria* (The pariah), a Paris-based Communist newspaper for Indigenous people from the colonies. Senghor's first article landed like a bombshell. As a decorated and disabled veteran, he chose to settle his scores with Blaise Diagne, the only African representative in the French Parliament during wartime. Diagne had recruited soldiers from the colonies by making false promises about equal treatment. But beyond the Black deputy, Senghor targeted the deceptive posturing of the French government: "France recognizes us when she needs our soldiers, but she continues to treat us like lesser creatures when the danger is past."

In the early 1920s, Lamine Senghor was a gift sent by heaven to the French Communist Party (PCF). Thanks to him and his comrades from North Africa and Indochina, the PCF was finally able to meet the demands of the Communist International, the Comintern. Based in Moscow, the organization required its affiliates "to assist all freedom movements in the colonies, not in words but in deeds."

To show the Comintern it was following directives, the PCF sponsored two candidates from the colonies in France's 1925 municipal elections. At first, Lamine Senghor hesitated to accept the nomination, not wanting to play the part of token Black man. In the end he accepted, hoping he could get across his anticolonial message. But when he wanted to speak about the thousands of native workers who died during the construction of the railroad from the Congo to the Atlantic coast, he was told to keep quiet. Lamine realized that the Communist Party might deplore the deaths in the colonies, but it was much more interested in the living conditions of French workers. ■

Lamine Senghor, French Army veteran, militant Communist and anticolonialist, and editor of the newspaper *The Pariah*.

Blaise Diagne, the first African member of France's Chamber of Deputies and the main voice of recruitment for the Senegalese tirailleurs.

Paris, Capital of Anticolonialism

Many students and intellectuals from the colonies lived in Paris, Geneva, Hamburg, Brussels, or London, but especially Paris. The French capital hosted, among others, M. N. Roy, from Bengal; Ho Chi Minh, from Vietnam; Messali Hadj, from Algeria; Zhou Enlai, from China; and Léopold Sédar Senghor, from Senegal. Drawn by the relative freedom of life in Paris, they took part in the birth of anti-imperialism. Paradoxically, anticolonial ideology and national awareness developed at the center of France's empire. Immigrants from the four corners of the world met there for the first time—natives of the West Indies, North Africa, sub-Saharan Africa, and Asia. They forged new alliances, shared seminal works of ideology, and traded practical knowledge about running a revolution or a republic. In the opening years of the twentieth century, nationalists expelled from the Indian subcontinent began to show up in Paris.

India House, founded in 1905 by Bhikaiji Rustom Cama, became one of the main focal points of Indian nationalism. Young intellectuals found underground military training there and published the anticolonialist journals the *Indian Sociologist* and *Bande Mataram*. In 1909, India House members published a manifesto urging all of Asia to join in political unity against the domination of the colonial powers: "Intellectuals of various Eastern nationalities can be found in Paris: Indians, Ottomans, Egyptians, Japanese, Chinese, Arabs, Armenians, Parsees, Persians, Siamese, and more. A pan-Asiatic parliament could easily be formed to coordinate the emancipation of the East…. A few Asian minds, sharpened in Paris, could mobilize 800 million swords. For too long Asia has dwelt in the darkness and in the shadow of death. Let us bring Asia together to form a unified entity, for unity will bring power."

In France, the colonizers adopted a more "civilized" attitude. They treated Indigenous immigrants with a tolerance and respect never seen in the colonies (mixed-race marriages were accepted, Blacks were addressed with the formal *vous*, etc.). The Peruvian Armando Bazán described the Latin Quarter in Paris as "a university of international encounters" that played a crucial role: the young Nguyen Ai Quoc, later to be known as Ho Chi Minh, spent a great deal of time in the Sainte Geneviève Library and met every week with activists from the West Indies, Africa, and Indochina at the restaurant "Le Pékin." In 1930, Paris's student population counted almost three hundred North Africans, more than eight hundred Vietnamese, and one thousand Chinese. The major figures of the pan-Asian and pan-African movements would come from their ranks.

Public Enemy Number One

Abd el-Krim's fighting men in the mountains of the Rif region

Having lost the first round, Lamine Senghor was bitter. He had gotten himself caught up in a political fight that concerned France and the French, a fight he had no stake in. It was time to refocus on the anticolonial struggle that was heating up again in several parts of the European empire. The most promising battlefield was right next to Europe, in the mountainous Rif region of northern Morocco. A traditional chieftain named Abd el-Krim al-Khattabi had managed to unify the tribal peoples to resist the Spanish and French invaders of their country. Writing in *Le Paria* in June 1925, Senghor gave voice to his dream: "From every point on earth, colonial peoples look at Abd el-Krim's victory and see the star that will lead them out of bondage."

LAMINE SENGHOR'S DREAM was the nightmare of the European powers. In 1921 Abd el-Krim's troops dealt the Spanish army a decisive defeat in the Moroccan town of Anoual. Sixteen thousand dead. Corpses lying under the sun for weeks, in gullies and on roadsides. Spaniards pored over photographs of the defeat in bewilderment. How had these tribes, described to them as primitive and disunited, managed to humiliate their military so completely? While Abd el-Krim's victory traumatized Spain, it was also a major worry for France. The two countries had divided Morocco between them in 1912, with Paris appropriating the bulk of the land area and ceding the mountains in the north, the Rif, to Madrid. Yet the Spanish now found it impossible to take possession of their share. Had this been happening in Patagonia or the Philippines, Spain's difficulties would have left France indifferent. But this was northern Morocco, right next to Algeria, the beating heart of France's empire. A large-scale revolt was not an option.

The mountains of the Rif region were a decided advantage to Abd el-Krim's fighting men as they engaged with the numerically superior Spanish colonial troops.

The Riffian army could just about stand up to the Spanish, but the French were another matter. If Abd el-Krim was to lead his people to safety, he'd have to innovate. Gain entry to the restrictive club of civilized nations. Found a nation worthy of the name. In 1923, he announced the formation of the Republic of the Rif. He reformed the legal and administrative system, built new schools, and laid out roads. The population was counted in a nationwide census, and military service was instituted. A new country had come into being, now to get it recognized.

A year earlier, in summer 1922, Abd el-Krim sent a letter to the European powers asking a blunt question: "Is there some racial or national prejudice that makes Europe exclude from its political community those suffering under the yoke of Spanish oppression?" No answer was ever forthcoming. When Abd el-Krim sent his emissaries to London and Paris, they held meetings with journalists, Communist Party leaders, and humanitarian figures, but no government official would consent to speak to them. Recognizing this disruptive Berber republic was out of the question. After all, if native groups started to create modern nation-states all on their own, then the whole concept of the civilizing mission collapsed. Justifying the colonial enterprise would be impossible.

From now on, nothing was off the table if it meant getting rid of the Republic of the Rif. The Spaniards, humiliated at Anoual, resorted to a weapon that the rest of Europe strongly disapproved of, mustard gas, dropping tons of it onto town squares and marketplaces in the Rif. Thousands of civilians were killed — men, women, and children. The goal was to terrorize the population and make Abd el-Krim surrender.

Spain's strategy was unsuccessful. Despite the horror of the chemical bombs, the Riffans didn't surrender an inch of their land. They held firmly to their territory. In the space of three years, Abd el-Krim became a hero from one end of Morocco to

The corpses of Spanish soldiers on Monte Arruit, where Abd el-Krim's army dealt the Spanish a decisive defeat at the battle of Anoual in July 1921.

another, admired by all. In fact, tribes that had been loyal to Paris up until then started siding with the Riffians.

At this point, Abd el-Krim posed a mortal danger to France. Wanting him out of the way once and for all, the French government sent General Pétain, the victor at the Battle of Verdun, with a gigantic army: 160,000 men, 250 airplanes, dozens of tanks, and hundreds of artillery pieces. Morocco had never seen a military force on this scale. To protect the lives of his people, Abd el-Krim surrendered to the French on May 26, 1926. He was deported to the French island of Réunion, where he spent the next twenty years, and gained asylum in Egypt, where he died in 1963. The Republic of the Rif was dead, but it had existed. That in itself was extraordinary. For five years, the Riffians had held two imperial powers at bay, showing what a determined population could do. The lesson was not lost on a younger generation of revolutionary leaders, from Ho Chi Minh to Che Guevara, who would study Abd el-Krim's saga.

To the anticolonial activists in Morocco and beyond, the price of freedom was becoming clear. They would have to organize, find allies, go on the attack. Strike on all fronts, using all available means, from armed combat to soccer field strategy, from religious tradition to Communist ideology. What was still hard to imagine was just how much the struggle would change them. ∎

Abd el-Krim, a Model for Revolutionaries Worldwide

"Flying over the Rif mountains, I looked out the airplane's portholes and saw that the region was ideal for guerrilla activities. It has become such a symbol." These words, in Spanish, were reportedly spoken by Ernesto "Che" Guevara to

Abd el-Krim when the two met in Cairo at a Moroccan embassy function on June 14, 1959. Che Guevara felt great admiration for the former leader of the Riffian rebellion, who had escaped from Réunion Island in 1947 and taken refuge in Egypt. There, he was looked upon as an elder statesman by the revolutionaries of the postwar period. The Rif War, which prompted like-minded movements all over the world, stood as the first anticolonial struggle of the twentieth century. At their training camp in Mexico, Che Guevara and Fidel and Raul Castro learned the subtleties of Abd el-Krim's guerrilla tactics from their instructor, Alberto Bayo, an officer and veteran of the Rif War, the son of a Spanish father and a Cuban mother who had gone to the Republican side during the Spanish Civil War. The story of the victory at Anoual on July 22, 1921 (known to Spanish historians as the "Anoual disaster"), made an impression on Fidel Castro. The guerrilla methods used by Abd el-Krim also inspired Ho Chi Minh and Mao Zedong. The disparity between the opposing forces in Morocco from 1920 to 1927, the asymmetry of the conflict, forced Abd el-Krim to adopt a strategy based on detailed knowledge of the terrain, light weapons, and high troop mobility. Vincent Sheean, a foreign correspondent for the *Chicago Tribune*, observed this new way of fighting firsthand and described it in a 1924 article:

> The strategy followed by Abd el-Krim and his brother was consistent: never engage in open battle except under extreme circumstances, but constantly harass, besiege, set up ambushes and fire at close range until the enemy feels demoralized and surrenders or beats a retreat before the invisible forces of Islam...The Abd el-Krim brothers made the fullest possible use of their fellow tribesmen, who lacked military training, by engaging in guerrilla warfare. Their goal was always to cut the enemy's lines of communication, make them think they were stronger than they actually were, and create a state of siege, both physical and psychological, that would eventually lead to surrender.

Many other fighters had used this strategy before, but Abd el-Krim was probably the first to apply it methodically and on a large scale.

2. Liberation
(1927–1954)

The Indigenous Internationale

Lamine Senghor with other delegates of the Anti-Imperialist Congress, Brussels, 1927

> The imperialist oppression that we call "colonization" in my country and that you call "imperialism" here is one and the same thing, comrades: it is all just capitalism.
>
> — LAMINE SENGHOR

MARSEILLES, 1926. An imperial city if there ever was one. Goods arrive here from the colonies: wine from Algeria, zinc from Indochina, peanuts from Senegal. And men come with them: Algerian workers, Southeast Asian sailors, Senegalese dockhands. For an activist on a mission, for Lamine Senghor, it's an ideal city. On September 4, 1926, he steps off the train at the Saint-Charles station determined to recruit new members for his growing political movement, the Committee for the Defense of the Negro Race.

As he's done in Le Havre and Bordeaux and at every stage of his tour, Lamine goes directly to the neighborhoods where Black dockworkers and laborers live, and he posts announcements of the public meetings he will be holding in local cafes. Whenever he encounters a group of workers from the colonies, he gets into a discussion with them, improvises a speech, tests out his ideas. Senghor rails against a world where Blacks are the lowest of the low. No one is going to step up and rescue them. The time has come to take ownership of the word "Negro." The time has come to turn the stigma around, make this contemptuous label a radiant symbol.

Lamine Senghor's speeches draw the attention of the colonial authorities and start to alarm them. For the whole two weeks he spends in Marseilles, the Senegalese militant is shadowed by an agent from the Colonial Ministry, a certain L. Josselme, who finds the man he is tailing quite impressive.

Since Senghor's arrival at the port of Marseilles, the native districts have become increasingly agitated, a fact I feel obliged to bring to your attention. Urgent measures, I believe, should be taken against this agitator to keep him from stepping up his pernicious propaganda, whose consequences could be dire.

— AGENT L. JOSSELME

The laborers, sailors, and longshoremen gather in greater numbers every night to hear Senghor. There are men from Senegal in his audience, of course, but also Madagascans, Algerians, and Indochinese. And white Communists. Although Senghor's focus is on freeing the Black man, he sticks close to the general message of the Communist International, the Comintern. Based in Moscow, the organization is more determined than ever to do away with imperialism. Capitalism will follow. Inevitably. And that task requires men like Lamine Senghor — professional revolutionaries from the European colonies.

Illustration by Lamine Senghor for his book *The Rape of a Country* (1927).

Lamine Senghor with other delegates of the Anti-Imperialist Congress in Brussels in February 1927.

In February 1927 Senghor arrives in Brussels, where he has been invited by the Comintern to attend the first World Anti-Imperialist Congress. Yet Senghor should not be traveling. His lungs were badly damaged by mustard gas at Verdun, and his condition is worsening. The handkerchief in his pocket is red from coughed-up blood. But the invitation was one he couldn't refuse. The list of delegates is a Who's Who of the anticolonial struggle: India's Jawaharlal Nehru, Indonesia's Mohammad Hatta, Algeria's Messali Hadj. There are also European activists — famous scientists, like Albert Einstein, and famous writers, like Romain Rolland and Maxim Gorky.

Climbing the stairs to the speaker's platform, Lamine Senghor ignores the piercing pain in his chest and the fever making his legs wobble. He starts by attacking the French colonial regime, with its claim to be civilizing the "Negroes" while at the same time refusing to educate them for fear they will rebel. He goes on to list the horrors inflicted on colonial subjects by their French masters: crushed testicles, floggings, and other tortures. His speech, which his audience listens to in silence, ends with his ringing denunciation of France's imperialism, which is nothing less than the oppression of its colonies for capitalist gain.

The speech is a sensation. Lamine Senghor is the breakout speaker at the congress. In anti-imperialist circles, his name is on all lips. His speech is translated into English, and its main points are debated even in the United States. In the wake of his experience, Senghor writes *The Rape of a Country*, a pamphlet that he illustrates himself. The book has a happy ending: poor whites join with native peoples to form "a fraternal alliance of free countries."

Lamine Senghor did not live to fight for his utopia. He died of tuberculosis in November 1927. He was thirty-eight years old. Banned by the French authorities, his book circulated underground in the colonies. It was read as far away as Dakar, by the native employees of Maurel et Prom, where Senghor had worked before going off to war, and where the flame of his rebellion had first been kindled. ■

The Civilizing Mission in Theory and Practice

The freedom fighters from the colonies who lived in France were quick to point out their government's contradictions. How could the French Republic so completely betray the ideals of its revolution, preaching equality and fraternity in Paris while subjugating Indigenous peoples overseas?

Thus the sovereignty enjoyed by the French people was not copied in most of the French empire, where a variety of local powers governed, watched over by colonial administrators. Secularism, an important principle of republican France, was also not extended to its overseas possessions. In Algeria, for instance, Muslims had no political or economic standing. This went against fundamental principles of French civil law, since it enshrined a distinction between citizens on the one hand and subjects on the other, a distinction completely antithetical to the universalist rights of man. We could draw a comparison with the situation in the United States, whose universalist ideology supported slavery and the Jim Crow laws. French colonists thereby excluded the colonized population from citizenship and because of their nationality subjected them to a separate set of laws. The Indigenous Peoples' Code of 1881, for instance, identified legal infractions that did not exist under French law and imposed collective penalties. Finally, the education given to the Indigenous population was very limited, for all that it was prominently featured in French colonial propaganda. Less than 10 percent of school-age children actually had the opportunity to attend school. This limited offer in fact corresponded to the tactic of summarily educating a small minority of the natives, who were then expected to support and assist the colonizers—without ever rising to become their equals.

Therefore the "civilizing mission" extolled by the French government since the 1880s to justify the colonizing project turned out to be a total hoax. The French Republic claimed it suppressed Indigenous customs and institutions in order to create a legal, administrative, and educational system that would assimilate the "natives." In fact, starting in the late nineteenth century, what developed in every corner of the French Empire—in Annam, Tonkin, Madagascar, and Morocco—were protectorates under the indirect rule of colonial administrators, a model inspired by the British Empire. It seems to have been a cheaper, more efficient way for the French to exercise control. Consequently, in the 1920s and 1930s Indigenous cultures were maintained under the influence of Orientalists, Africanists, and scholars of colonial science who tended to defend policies that preserved the local social and administrative structures—whose study, not coincidentally, was their bread and butter. For colonial subjects, it didn't seem to matter where they turned, they always ended up in the same place.

The Stronger Sex

Friends, I come to you from many thousand miles away, as the ambassador of a very ancient country to the youngest nation in the world. It may surprise you that a country that you are taught to regard as conservative could have chosen a woman to be its representative and ambassador. But if you read aright the whole history of Indian civilization, you will realize that woman has been the very pivot and inspiration of its culture. What my country says to you, in the words of the old Hindu prayer that rises up in every home night after night: *Shanti, shanti, shanti.* Peace, peace, peace.

— SAROJINI NAIDU

NEW YORK, 1928. It's here that the wealth and power of the world are concentrated. It's here that the battles over the future are decided. And it's to New York that Sarojini Naidu comes, disembarking one October morning. A charismatic poet and political leader, Naidu hadn't wanted to leave India, where the struggle against the British Empire was gaining strength every day. But people insisted she was the only person who could wipe away the smear, the only person who could convince the Americans that no, India wasn't barbaric. That yes, India deserved its independence. So Naidu came. It had all started a year earlier with a book, *Mother India,* by the American journalist Katherine Mayo, in which India was described as one of the circles of hell. A doomed country under the spell of a backward religion, Hinduism. A sick nation unable to produce healthy citizens. It was clear to Katherine Mayo that such primitive people were not yet ready for independence. Without the British, they would be lost. The book was a sensation. But Indian nationalists needed American help, and so they had to counterattack.

A day after stepping off the boat, Sarojini Naidu faced the Fox Movietone cameras and made her case against Mayo's outrageous thesis.

A graduate of Cambridge University and a leader of the self-rule movement, celebrated for her poems in Bengali, Hindi, and English, Sarojini Naidu fascinated the American people. Her voice succeeded in convincing her audience that India needed to be freed from British rule, just as the American colonies had in earlier times. For eight months, she traveled the country, stopping at every church and university, from the most progressive to the most conservative.

Sarojini Naidu did not make her case only to white audiences, to those in power. She stepped through the looking glass and explored Black America as well. What she found moved her to tears as she visited sites ranging from the shanty towns of Chicago to the campus of Howard University. She saw the Black population as the untouchables of America. At home in India, where she was a Brahman, she had broken with tradition to marry a man of lower caste. She hadn't expected to find pariahs in the United States too. In the India of the future, untouchables would no longer exist. But for that to happen, she needed to return to her country and take up the struggle again.

Now that she had defended her country's honor in a foreign land, Sarojini Naidu would fight for her sisters, the forgotten women of India — the widows, the unmarried, the women killed over a dowry dispute, the girls married off at age nine. Naidu had traveled, studied. She had led the Indian National Congress, the biggest political party in the country. But this was just her personal destiny, an individual career that had done nothing to change the lives of 150 million Indian women. The time had come to shift to a higher gear.

To do this, she would have to turn to her old friend Gandhi, the spiritual leader of the Indian nationalist movement. In late

Sarojini Naidu leading the march toward the Dharasana salt factory, May 1930.

March 1930, the mahatma set out on a march to the sea to protest the British monopoly on salt. The colonial administration had placed a high tax on salt, making it exceedingly expensive in India, a tax that fell unfairly on India's poorest and robbed their lives of savor. Gandhi walked for 240 miles, gathering tens of thousands of marchers along the way — all of them men. Not a single woman marched at his side.

But when he reached the last stage of his march, Sarojini Naidu joined him. She accompanied him everywhere and stood beside him while the cameras clicked. Her presence triggered an unprecedented response. Women came by the thousands from every side. They collected salt from the coastal salt flats, enacting the largest campaign of civil disobedience the world had ever seen. Women proved themselves as freedom fighters on an equal footing with men. When Gandhi was arrested a month later by

Sarojini Naidu beside her friend and political leader Mohandas Karamchand Gandhi.

the colonial administration, he very naturally turned over the leadership of his movement to Sarojini Naidu. It was she who would lead the marchers to the saltworks at Dharasana. This was a dangerous enterprise, a deliberate provocation that would force the British to commit irreparable acts of retaliation. On the morning of May 21, 1930, she addressed the marchers: "The body of Gandhi is in prison, but his soul is at our side. India's good name is in your hands. You must not use any violence under any circumstances. You will be beaten but you must not resist: you must not even raise a hand to ward off blows."

One after another, the protesters fell at the feet of the armed policemen. By the end of the day, there were 320 injured and two dead. Naidu was arrested with hundreds of other militants. The United Press correspondent wrote an account that excoriated the British. His article was reprinted in 1,350 newspapers around the world. For the British Raj, this represented a devastating blow. And it had been dealt by a woman. ■

"Being Able to Say No": The Unstoppable Power of Disobedience

Colonization by the Western powers has almost always coincided with a continuing military and administrative substructure. In other words, a tiny minority of colonizers could never rule over the vast majority of an Indigenous population. Consequently, Europeans recruited large numbers of "native" agents into the army, the police, and the administration. But coercion was not enough on its own. Colonizers tried to give their rule legitimacy by gaining the consent of a subset of their subjects, using various forms of inducement and recompense. Colonial rule was impossible without the cooperation of at least a fraction of the population and the local elites, who made use of the foreign presence to buttress their own social and economic position. Following a divide-and-conquer strategy, colonial administrations would favor certain groups over others, such as the Brahmins in India, the *priyayi* in the Dutch East Indies, and the Tutsi in Rwanda, whom they relied on to maintain the social order to the detriment of the rest of the population. Gandhi spoke out against cooperation specifically, holding that the first step to emancipation and decolonization was for Indians to stop cooperating with the British colonizer:

> The [present] government has no power except through the co-operation, willing or forced, of the people. The force it exercises is given it entirely by our own people. One lakh of Europeans, without our help, could not hold even one-seventh of our villages...A nation of 350 million people does not need the dagger of the assassin, it does not need the poison bowl, it does not need the sword, the spear or the bullet. It needs simply a will of its own, an ability to say "no," and that nation is today learning to say "no."

Starting in South Africa in 1906 where, as a young lawyer, he defended Indians, Gandhi began to practice *satyagraha*, or "truth force," in the form of campaigns of nonviolent resistance that included a mixture of demonstrations, strikes, civil disobedience, and the boycott of British products. In the first half of the twentieth century, colonial subjects like the Egyptian nationalists in 1914 and the Koreans of the March 1st Movement in 1919 put these new political tactics to work and slowly but surely undermined foreign rule.

From Hong Kong with Love

Ho Chi Minh, Vietnamese revolutionary and statesman

> The path to Paris and London goes through the cities of Afghanistan, the Punjab, and Bengal.
>
> — LEON TROTSKY

WHENEVER he had a moment to himself, Nguyen Ai Quoc wrote to his wife. A few lines, simple and straightforward, to express his loneliness, his sense of loss, his pain: "I'm taking advantage of this opportunity to send you a few words of reassurance. Though we have been separated now for almost a year, our feelings for each other need not be spoken to be felt."

The letter was intercepted by the French political police and never reached its intended reader. Nguyen Ai Quoc, the Comintern's best agent in Southeast Asia, would never see his beloved again. And he would never remarry. From now on he would be wedded to the revolution. Constantly on the move, he traveled between China, Siam, Hong Kong, and Malaysia. He managed to stay under the radar of the British and Chinese police by disguising himself as a Chinese trader or a Buddhist priest from Thailand. The French, for their part, had long since identified him as a dangerous enemy, a person who could someday make them lose the pearl of the empire — the country they called Indochina but that its patriots knew as Vietnam.

The agents of the French political police first put Nguyen under surveillance when he founded the Communist newspaper *Le Paria* (The pariah) in Paris in the early 1920s. They then tracked him moving to Moscow, where they lost his scent. They knew he had been prowling around Vietnam. The rebel farmers were talking about him, and Communist ideas were gaining ground. Unable to capture Nguyen, the French condemned him to

On September 2, 1945, Ho Chi Minh announced the creation of the Democratic Republic of Vietnam.

death in absentia, but it seemed to have no effect. Nguyen continued to organize the struggle from neighboring countries. So that those who'd rebelled before would not have died in vain. So that past defeats would not happen again.

Nguyen Ai Quoc was an adolescent during the first big anti-colonial revolt, a time when the colonists sent postcards back to their fiancées in Dijon or Marseilles featuring the severed heads of rebels. He learned a big lesson from that defeat. If the Vietnamese wanted to kick the French out, they had to collect around a single banner, the banner of the Communist Party.

In February 1930, Nguyen Ai Quoc gathered all the most committed activists together in Hong Kong, a British territory. The Chinese New Year was being noisily celebrated in the streets, but the activists paid no attention. Together, in the space of four days, they created the Vietnamese Communist Party. Just in time, because the whole country from the far North to the South was in a state of upheaval. Nguyen Ai Quoc assigned his comrades to fan out and assume the leadership of the rebellion. But the French colonial administration was determined to crush the political movement from the outset. The French air force bombed the rebel villages into oblivion. The leaders of the Communist Party were arrested one after another and sentenced to prison or capital punishment.

Having stayed behind in Hong Kong to coordinate the rebellion, Nguyen Ai Quoc was identified by the British police. On June 6, 1931, he was arrested for subversive activities. The English were unsure what to do with their troublesome prisoner, whom the Comintern was insisting they set free and whom the French were eager to execute. In the end, they quietly smuggled him out of Hong Kong and sent him to Shanghai, where he found passage

Chinese nationalists executed for having poisoned French soldiers in northern Tonkin, Indochina, 1908.

to Communist Russia. Eight years later, the Vietnamese leader would return to his country and resume the fight against colonization. He would no longer be known as Nguyen Ai Quoc but as Ho Chi Minh. In Vietnamese, it means "bright spirit." ∎

Secret Agents Working Toward Decolonization

In May 1913, inspired by the revolutionary movements in China, the Ottoman Empire, and Persia, Lenin wrote an article called "Backward Europe and Progressive Asia." On a similar note, in 1919 Trotsky wrote, "The path to Paris and London goes through the cities of Afghanistan, the Punjab, and Bengal." The Bolsheviks were absolutely certain that, if the revolution was to be permanent, it would need to be worldwide. That's why they founded the Communist International, or Comintern, in 1919. This new organization brought together Indigenous activists from the colonies who, in the wake of the October Revolution, set out to rid the world of imperialism and capitalism. In those early years, the Russian revolutionaries were still advocating militant anticolonialism and had given up control over several territories such as Finland and Estonia that had been pre–World War I dependencies of the Russian Empire. They unequivocally upheld the right to self-determination of peoples in Europe's colonial possessions. Hundreds of young activists—among them the Vietnamese Ho Chi Minh, the Chinese Deng Xiaoping, the Kenyan Jomo Kenyatta, and the Indonesian Tan Malaka—were educated in the Comintern's Moscow schools, including the famous Communist University of the Toilers of the East. They then went on to play decisive roles in spreading the ideology of the Third International. One such activist was the Bengali Manabendra Nath Roy, who in 1919 founded the Communist Party of Mexico and a year later the Communist Party of India while in exile in Uzbekistan.

All of these experienced agents had a number of pseudonyms and a corresponding number of passports, enabling them to travel throughout the European empires incognito. Asia became a strategic priority after the failure of the German revolution in 1923. The colonial powers quickly organized to combat the influence of the Comintern's agents and their new followers. The British established an anti-Bolshevist commission in India that harshly repressed Communist activists in the years between the two world wars. A number of these intellectuals, however, distanced themselves from the Communists, starting in the mid-1920s. Lamine Senghor reproached his European comrades for not paying enough attention to the fate of the Indigenous peoples of sub-Saharan Africa, while M. N. Roy broke with the Comintern in 1929, after it was brutally taken over by Stalin.

The Battle Over Caste

Bhimrao Ramji Ambedkar

Unfortunately, I was born an untouchable. There is nothing I can do about that. But I can refuse to live under these humiliating conditions. It is time to put an end to this harassment and vilification. Let us abolish this system of castes that makes us into vermin. Let us choose a new religion that will offer us an equal chance. I was born a Hindu, but I can solemnly swear to you that I will not die a Hindu!

— BHIMRAO RAMJI AMBEDKAR

BHIMRAO RAMJI AMBEDKAR was an untouchable. From the very start he had to fight for the right to exist. In the early 1930s he was the most brilliant intellectual in British India, the recipient of multiple diplomas. By birth, though, he had been destined for another life entirely, one steeped in death, excrement, blood, and filth. The untouchable's lot in India is just that: impurity. Other Hindus may neither touch them nor come near them. If they do, they risk being reincarnated as untouchables themselves. A neatly regulated system. A system that Ambedkar wanted to break up once and for all.

To do this he didn't hesitate to use the British. Following the Salt March, the British government no longer had any choice. It had to loosen its grip, organize elections, share the power. Faithful to their maxim of "Divide and rule," the English offered to reserve some seats in the legislature for untouchables. Gandhi was against the proposal, Ambedkar was for it. Gandhi went on a hunger strike. Ambedkar stood his ground. Gandhi gave in.

This was a step in the right direction, but it would change nothing in the daily life of untouchables. Ambedkar had made Gandhi fall into step, but he would now need to get the Hindu traditionalists on his side as well. And use the strongest methods to do so.

There is always a tipping point. The words were lined up in his head, but all his experiences came crowding back to him as he prepared to speak. The victories, the humiliations. The two doctorates he'd been awarded, one in London and one in New York. The thousand and one times he'd been refused a simple glass of water. It was October 13, 1935, and Dr. Bhimrao Ramji Ambedkar was prepared to make the ultimate transgression.

Determined to put an end to the discrimination he faced as a Hindu untouchable, he announced his intention to convert to Islam and to encourage all of India's untouchables to follow suit.

In 1930, 50 million Indians were Dalits, or untouchables.

On October 13, 1935, Bhimrao Ramji Ambedkar, speaking at Yeola, called for the abolition of the caste system.

Ambedkar had just dropped a bombshell. In India, where there is constant tension between proponents of the country's two dominant faiths, Hinduism and Islam, no subject is more explosive than religion. The conservatives were quick to calculate the political consequences. If fifty million untouchables converted to Islam all at once, Hindus would lose their political ascendancy. To keep this nightmare from happening, some concessions were in order. On November 12, 1936, in Travancore at the extreme southern tip of India, Hindu temples were opened to untouchables for the first time. The following year, in Bombay, untouchables were allowed to drink from public fountains. Ambedkar promised himself that he would build on these local victories and incorporate them into national law the moment India won its independence. He'd achieved his goal of making the untouchables central elements of Indian society. The India of tomorrow would have to make room for them.

For now, though, the British were still in India. And they were not yet ready even to consider granting India its independence. It was still too early. It's always too early. Just then another European war loomed on the horizon. To win it Great Britain would need India to send soldiers into the line of fire. Again. ■

Subhas Chandra Bose: A Founding Father of Modern-Day India

European historians have traditionally been drawn to analogies: the Trung sisters, for instance, who led a rebellion against the Chinese in the first century AD, have been called the "Vietnamese Joans of Arc"; and Qianlong, emperor of the Qing Dynasty in the eighteenth century, is often referred to as the "Chinese Louis XIV." By contrast, other comparisons have been off-limits: no one in Europe has yet dared compare Subhas Chandra Bose to General de Gaulle. With some jus-tification, because the two men belonged to opposite sides during World War II. Yet from the Indian perspective, particularly as Hindu nationalism gains ground in India's northern half, Bose is considered one of the founding fathers of the nation. While Gandhi and Nehru advocated pacifism, Bose proposed another way of decolonizing India: armed struggle. Married to an Austrian woman, Emi-lie Schenkl, he traveled widely in Europe before becoming leader of the Indian National Congress party, from 1938 to 1939. The outbreak of the war gave him the chance to undertake his project of winning back his country by force of arms. In early 1941 Bose went to Berlin where he enlisted several thousand Indians, former prisoners of war and students living in Germany, to join an Indian fight-ing force. Formed as a division of the Wehrmacht, the India Legion was intended to free India from British subjugation. Despite its stated purpose, however, the legion remained in Europe, stationed at various times in Germany, Holland, and on the Atlantic coast of France. Unhappy with Hitler, Bose turned to the other major Axis power, Japan. In Tokyo he took command of the new Indian National Army, composed mainly of Indian soldiers of the British army captured at the fall of Singapore in 1942. Among the soldiers were coolies who had worked on plan-tations and a large number of women, who formed the only all-female combat unit outside the USSR—it was known as the Rani of Jhansi Regiment, after the nineteenth-century heroine of the Indian independence movement. On October 21, 1943, Bose founded Azad Hind, the Provisional Government of Free India, with the military and financial support of the Japanese. Headquartered in Sin-gapore, this government had its own army, its own currency, and its own judicial system and civil code. It claimed authority over all Indian civilians and military personnel in the former British colonies of Southeast Asia and in any lands con-trolled by the Japanese and the Indian National Army. Thus, starting in 1943, the Government of Free India was briefly able to rule over the Andaman and Nico-bar Islands, and over parts of Manipur and Nagaland. This political experiment ended suddenly with Bose's death in an airplane accident on August 18, 1945, followed two weeks later by Japan's surrender.

Determined to Write

Algerian writer Kateb Yacine

The war was over. The Nazis had been defeated. The bells rang out, and everyone joined the celebration. A rumor immediately started that we would be given our freedom the next day. So it was a day of vast hope for all Algerians. And on the morning of May 8, there was a big demonstration, a huge crowd. I recognized classmates among the demonstrators. They waved at me, and without really knowing what it was all about I thought, I'll go watch the parade. Then I started to hear gunshots.

— KATEB YACINE

TO BE FIFTEEN YEARS OLD, to live in the town of Sétif, in French Algeria. To be called Yacine and go to high school. To have one's life ahead of one. To dream. To write. To imagine oneself a poet, like one's grandfather, the aptly named Si-Ahmed El Ghazali Kateb. Because *kateb*, in Arabic, means "writer." To imagine oneself a poet, maybe, but in a different language — in French, the language of Baudelaire and Rimbaud. The language also of one's schoolteachers Mademoiselle Dubac and Mademoiselle Clément, whom it was impossible not to have a crush on. To love this language, even if it belongs to the colonists. This language that frees you from your family, lets you cut the cord.

Lighthearted and carefree, Yacine is strolling through the streets of Sétif. The Allied forces have defeated Germany. He's happy, like everyone else. It's market day. Villagers have come into town from other parts of the region. It's market day and, in a flash, everything is going to change — both Yacine's life and the fate of Algeria.

That's when he hears gunshots, just as he's preparing to join his friends at the demonstration.

Screams, shouts, explosions, bodies falling to the ground. Chaos like Yacine has never seen. The flag bloodied. This was the flag of the newly reconceived Algeria, the flag of the rural population, the militants, the Muslim scouts. And it was Yacine's flag from now on. It was this flag, in fact, that had triggered the policemen's fury. *This land is part of France, you numbskulls, so think again*, they seemed to be saying. *We may have beaten the Nazis, but is that any reason for you to get your country back?* There was mayhem in the streets of Sétif. The Europeans were firing into the crowd. The Algerians were killing any Frenchman they could get their hands on. Dodging bullets, Yacine returned to his village. But already the army was distributing guns to the colonists. It was open season on the Indigenous population.

> *The army occupied the village, the whole region, then on May 13, they came for me at home. They were civilians. I was arrested and taken to the police station. Then to Sétif, to the artillery camp there, where about six thousand of us were gathered. Some were younger than me, some were only twelve years old, kids they'd picked up. They really wanted to destroy us, they were targeting the youth of Algeria. All the young people who were raising their heads. They knew the young were raising their heads, and they reacted in an extreme way. Really...you would never have suspected there was so much hatred. So a lot of my classmates, a lot of the young people that I was close to and a lot of others were arrested and coldly executed by the militia.*

> **— KATEB YACINE**

Killing schoolchildren, killing militants, killing farmers. Punishment, punishment, punishment. Crushing the revolt in the egg so that Algeria would go on being French. So that the fiction main-tained for more than a century could be perpetuated.

Algeria was not a colony. It was three départements, three administrative regions of France. The same inscriptions carved on the town halls in every village and town in France adorned the town halls there: *Liberté, égalité, fraternité*. Yes, but it meant freedom, equality, and brotherhood for the 900,000 French cit-izens only. A different set of principles applied to the 7.5 million Muslims — and to them alone. Submission on a daily basis. And if this system was to endure, the little troublemakers like Yacine had to be executed. But death didn't want him. Someone had to write the story.

Kabyle farmers arrested in the Setif region of Algeria after the uprising of May 8, 1945.

French colonials distributing weapons and forming a militia in Guelma, Algeria.

Being fifteen in Algeria. Surviving and embracing one's destiny. Taking over the words of Mademoiselle Dubac, the words of Mademoiselle Clément. Describing the world then in its death throes. Announcing the world to come. Writing *Nedjma* (1956), a novel that takes place in the east of Algeria, during the period following the Sétif massacre. Becoming Kateb Yacine, founder of modern Algerian literature. ■

Colonization without Colonists?

"White" colonies are the exception. Apart from the thirteen American colonies, we can count them on the fingers of one hand: Canada, Australia, and New Zealand. These could be called "new Britains," and they were peopled fairly quickly by a European majority and achieved political autonomy within the British Empire in the late nineteenth century. These colonies became "white" only because the Indigenous peoples (apart from the Maoris) were effectively obliterated. But in most colonial territories, the colonizers—counting both those who were there temporarily as administrators or soldiers and those who were born there—formed a small fraction of the population. In many parts of the world, the Indigenous peoples never saw whites but dealt instead with their Indigenous representatives. In the 1930s, colonials in British India numbered 160,000 and accounted for 0.04 percent of the population; the 25,000 colonials in Indochina accounted for 0.1 percent of the population; and the 16,000 colonials in French West Africa also accounted for 0.1 percent of the population. Because of their sparse representation, the European colonial powers often kept the Indigenous administrative structures in place (royal governments, chieftainships, etc.). The demographics of the only true "settlement colony" in the French Empire, Algeria, reflect the limited extent of colonial emigration. The French made up only half of the 400,000 Europeans (10 percent of the total population) living in Algeria in 1880; the remainder were Spaniards and Balearic Islanders in the towns of western Algeria and Italians and Maltese in the east. The European colonizers jealously guarded the vote for themselves until World War II, which brought about the first significant increase in political power for the Algerians. At that point, Algeria had 8.5 million inhabitants, of whom 950,000 were Europeans, mostly in the cities of Algiers, Constantine, and Oran. The decrees of March 7, 1944, and August 17, 1945, gave all male Muslims over the age of twenty-one (numbering 1,210,000) the right to vote in elections for a second assembly, equal in weight to the common law assembly. The French and Algerian communities would then each be represented by twenty-two parliamentary representatives. This last gasp subterfuge, invented by the colonizers to neutralize the democratic claims of the Algerian people, was quickly shown to be hollow. The law of February 5, 1958, establishing a single parliamentary assembly, however, came much too late. The time for "colonial reform" was long past.

Breaking Away

Gandhi arrives at Simla, 1945

The time is here and now when we stand up and say, "We take up the challenge" to those who defied Mahatma Gandhi. We are his living symbols. We are his soldiers. We are the carriers of his banner before an embattled world. Our banner is truth. Our shield is nonviolence. Our sword is a sword of the spirit that conquers without blood.

— SAROJINI NAIDU

NEW DELHI, AUGUST 15, 1947. All her adult life, Sarojini Naidu has fought for this moment. Victory, freedom. Independence for India! And it is she, the poet, who steps up to the microphones at the newly minted national radio service to give the official speech. In lyrical tones, she praises her friend Gandhi, the prophet of nonviolence, the general who brought victory. A tiny man, he managed to lead a successful revolution that, for the first time in history, involved no bloodletting. Gandhi, nonviolence, a common humanity. These words and images are uttered to blot out the horrible visions crowding Sarojini's consciousness.

The partition, the massacres.

Flashback. Two years earlier, in June 1945, the British had thrown in the towel. Worn down by decades of civil disobedience, they finally promised to leave India. This raised the question of how many nations would come into being to replace of the old colony.

India has hundreds of languages and a multiplicity of religions and castes. Yet only two of its religious groups were openly and incessantly in conflict: the Hindus and the Muslims. The first wanted to impress their stamp on the India of tomorrow; the second were afraid of being completely wiped out. Most Hindus

Indian refugees flee the violence in East Punjab after the partition of India and the creation of Pakistan (1947).

voted for the Indian National Congress, which was Gandhi's party and Sarojini Naidu's. They wanted a unified India, and they promised Muslims that they would be protected and provided for. Most Muslims, though, rallied to Ali Jinnah, the leader of the All-India Muslim league. Jinnah did not believe Gandhi's promises. He wanted to create a new and separate state, Pakistan, in the two parts of the country where Muslims formed the majority.

The British, now that they'd made up their minds, were in a hurry to leave. They gathered the major players in Indian politics together in Simla, the British administration's summer capital, a jewel of colonial architecture. Everyone smiled for the camera, but behind closed doors acrimony reigned. The tension between Gandhi and Jinnah was palpable. The British had spent three centuries sowing discord to consolidate their own power and were unable to quell factional quarrels now. That left only one solution: partition.

It was the greatest divorce in the history of mankind, and it wasn't likely to be amicable. Hindus and Muslims killed each other from one end of the country to the other. It broke Gandhi's heart. He'd managed to make the English leave using peaceful means, but now he couldn't stop his own countrymen from killing each other. Yet he didn't give up. Traveling to the massacre sites, he preached reconciliation to the surviving Hindus and Muslims. A desperate plea.

On August 15, 1947, Pakistan and India officially separated and became independent. Those who found themselves on the wrong side of the border had to scramble madly. The Hindus and Sikhs who didn't leave Pakistan quickly enough were brutally massacred. The Muslims who didn't flee Northern India in time were assassinated in droves. In all, five hundred thousand people died.

Mahatma Gandhi, leader of the Indian National Congress party, and Ali Jinnah, president of the Muslim League, during the negotiations at Simla in 1944.

Fourteen million refugees managed to cross the borders alive. Gandhi did not celebrate India's independence, he spent his time with the refugees, spreading his message of peace. The Muslims are our brothers, we are all Indians. This message infuriated Hindu extremists, and it particularly infuriated a man named Nathuram Godse.

As far as Godse was concerned, Gandhi was clearly working for the Muslims. If India was ever to become truly Hindu, Gandhi had to die. On January 30, 1948, at evening prayer, Godse approached the mahatma. As a devout Hindu, he bowed to him, then straightened up, drew his gun, and pulled the trigger. One version of India died, and a different one came into being.

Two days later, it was Sarojini Naidu, Gandhi's longtime friend, who spoke his funeral oration on All India Radio, the same network where, in lyrical tones, she had rejoiced in India's independence. Now she called on all Indians to continue Gandhi's struggle, wielding the shield of nonviolence and the spirit sword that conquers without blood. ◼

1947: Forgotten Independences

The political geography of the Indian subcontinent could have taken a very different turn at the time of decolonization. The line marking the border between the Dominion of India and Pakistan was greatly complicated by the integration of the 562 princely states, which together accounted for 40 percent of India's land area. Although the British and India's nationalist leaders promised to guarantee the internal autonomy of these states, several of the rulers refused to join either of the two new countries. On the Pakistani side, the khan of Khalat in Baluchistan announced his state's independence on August 15, 1947, and the Pakistani army was forced to annex his kingdom on April 1, 1948. In India the nawab of Junagadh chose to side with Pakistan, though 60 percent of his 670,000 subjects were Hindus. Concerned with the effect of this precedent on other Muslim rulers, India invaded Junagadh on November 9, 1947. The very powerful nizam of Hyderabad, a Muslim, who ruled a large state at the center of the subcontinent, declared Hyderabad's independence, overriding the will of his Hindu subjects who accounted for 86 percent of the state's 17 million people. The Indian government penalized the openly pro-Pakistani nizam by putting Hyderabad under economic blockade. The nizam appealed to the United Nations in August 1948, and India's prime minister, Jawaharlal Nehru, forcibly invaded the state, killing eight hundred of the nizam's soldiers.

The international community reacted with indignation to this show of force and watched closely the brewing situation in the kingdom of Jammu and Kashmir, where the maharajah Hari Singh, a Hindu, reigned over a largely Muslim population. This region lies between India, Pakistan, Afghanistan, Xinjiang Province in China, and Tibet. Hari Singh hesitated over whether to declare his state independent, a move that at least part of the population favored. While he delayed in coming to an official decision, uprisings broke out, which were co-opted by the Muslim movement of free Kashmir. Singh moved to suppress the insurrections, but on October 22, 1947, Pakistani paramilitary forces started to lend their support to the rebels. Under pressure, Singh chose to integrate his state with India, and Indian reinforcements arrived on October 27 to bring Kashmir back under control. This began the first armed conflict between India and Pakistan over a region that both sides claimed and whose fate is still in contention today, seventy years later. Meanwhile, under cover of the hostilities between India and Pakistan, the French and the Portuguese were able to maintain their trading posts in Pondicherry and Goa for another decade.

Wambui's Oath

Suspected Mau Mau fighters being searched by British security forces

Not surprisingly, one of the responses to prolonged exploitation was the development of underground groups dedicated to the violent overthrow of the colonial overlords. And if the utopian vision animating these groups would eventually have to reckon with reality, with fallibility, with human imperfection, this could be dealt with at a later time. The first order of business was to remove the occupier.

THE YEAR IS 1952. Wambui Waiyaki is sixteen years old. She attends the girls' school in Mambere, in Kikuyu country, in British Kenya. Wambui likes the Scots missionary sisters who teach her class. She gets along with them well, except when they insist that she go by her baptismal name, Virginia. Her name is Wambui. Her great-grandfather was Waiyaki wa Hinga, a great chieftain of the Kikuyu, a proud African. He made trouble for the whites, so they killed him. Then they seized his territory. Though it happened sixty years ago, Wambui is determined to avenge her great-grandfather one day.

And that day is at hand. The day of her oath. For some time Wambui has been hearing about this mysterious movement, the Mau Mau. They are Kikuyus in revolt against the colonists. More than any other people in Kenya, the Kikuyus have seen their lives disrupted by colonization. The English chose their territory to create a fabulous country for themselves, a country of gentleman farmers, tea parties, and safaris. A country where one million Blacks work for sixty thousand whites. A country that the Mau Mau want to reclaim.

To do this they need to band together. In the days of Wambui's great-grandfather, young Kikuyu men took an oath of loyalty to the group on becoming adults. It is this oath that the Kikuyu reinvent to bring their people together. Strengthen them to challenge the colonials. And since the struggle affects everyone, this time women will also take the oath. On this day in 1952, Wambui wonders what will happen to her on entering the darkened hut. But she is determined to endure anything. What she goes through here is nothing compared to what the English will inflict on her if they catch her one day.

First, Wambui is slapped in the face. She takes it. Then she is made to drink a mouthful of sacred liquid. It is foul but symbolic, made of blood and dirt. Wambui is proud, brave. She has met all the tests to which she has been subjected. She swears to fight to regain the land that the whites have taken from the Kikuyu. She swears to steal weapons and kill all enemies of the movement, even her brother if need be. She swears never to speak about the oath. On penalty of death.

Wambui is now a combatant. Without a word to her family, she quits school and leaves her village. She goes to Nairobi where she throws herself heart and soul into the cause. She is sixteen, speaks good English, and is a Christian. From the British point of view, she is above suspicion. Working under their noses, she sets up a network of drivers, watchmen, household servants, and prostitutes. The goal is to penetrate the colonials' houses, steal their money and documents. Inebriate the soldiers of the colonial army, get hold of their weapons. Put all of this into the hands of the Mau Mau combatants in the forest. Celebrate when they attack a police station or kill a pro-British leader. This is Wambui's life, a life in complete opposition to the life envisioned for her by the Scots missionary nuns.

Every day her life grows more dangerous. Swept up in a raid, Wambui is interrogated by the colonial police. She plays up her youth and good breeding and manages to talk the British into releasing her. But hundreds of thousands of Kikuyus are being picked up in government dragnets, both in Nairobi and in the

Kikuyus in the British "rehabilitation" camp in Langata at the height of the repressive campaign against the Mau Mau independence movement.

villages. Mass arrests intended to root out the insurrectionary evil. As far as the colonials are concerned, the Mau Maus don't represent a revolt. No, it's a sickness, a madness, a collective psychosis. How else to explain that the Kikuyu are refusing to accept the progress, the "civilization," of the British?

Madness has to be addressed. The "evil" at its root has to be attacked. One million Kikuyus pass through internment camps, where they are sorted into three colors: white for those who've been rehabilitated, gray for those undergoing reeducation, and black for the irredeemable. To get to white, you have to confess your sin, admit that you belong to the rebellion. Then you have to take a new oath meant to supersede the Mau Mau one.

A period of reapprenticeship to Christian values and civilization then follows. And to make sure the teaching has been truly absorbed, it is accompanied by torture, rape, and sometimes castration. And malnutrition, invariably. Unbelievable violence. But a violence seen as therapeutic by the colonials. A violence responsible for the deaths of tens of thousands of men, women, and children.

Those who survive this process aren't exactly home free. There are 845 new villages created to receive them. Villages surrounded by a ditch and guarded by armed men. The graduates of these camps are meant to be a regenerated people. Who understand, finally, that the whites want only what's good for them.

But it doesn't work. The British defeat the Mau Mau, but they do not break the spirit of the Kikuyu. Nor of the other Kenyans. In the end the British have to grant Kenya its independence in 1963: the new Republic is led by Jomo Kenyatta. And in this new country, Wambui becomes a prominent female politician. She spends the rest of her life fighting sexism, tribalism, and the one-party system. So that the country she believes in can someday rise to the level of her girlhood dreams. ■

Presumed Mau Mau insurgents being led to trial in Githunguri, Kenya, on April 16, 1953.

The Mau Mau Rebellion as Seen by Others

At a rally in Harlem in December 1964, Malcolm X had this to say:

> The Mau Mau will go down as the greatest African patriots and freedom fighters that that continent ever knew, and they will be given credit for bringing about the independence of many of the existing independent states on that continent right now...You and I can best learn how to get real freedom by studying how Kenyatta brought it to his people in Kenya...In fact, that's what we need in Mississippi. In Mississippi we need a Mau Mau. In Alabama we need a Mau Mau. In Georgia we need a Mau Mau. Right here in Harlem, in New York City, we need a Mau Mau.

On the other hand, some African-American leaders saw the Mau Mau as a threat to social order. They rightly understood that the Mau Mau were fighting not only British rule but also the traditional power of the Kikuyu. As evidence they pointed to the fact that the overwhelming majority of civilians killed by the rebels (1,822 out of 1,880) were Blacks. The Pulitzer Prize–winning journalist Malcolm Johnson, for instance, writing in *The Defender* and the *Atlanta Daily World*, denounced the Mau Mau as a "terrorist group," whose members "buy their wives and sell their daughters in exchange for cattle." The US government itself, as represented by the undersecretary of state J. C. Satterthwaite, hesitated between supporting anticolonialism and defending against the possibility of revolution: "We support African political aspirations when they are moderate, non-violent, and constructive.... We also support Africa's ties with Western Europe" (1959). By casting the movement as "a small rebellion led by bloodthirsty savages," the British had robbed it of its political legitimacy in the court of public opinion throughout most of the world. Except for a few countries, mainly the Soviet Union and India, who voiced their support for the African rebels, the world as a whole seemed afraid that the spark of the Mau Mau rebellion might set all of Africa on fire.

Endgame

Viet Minh soldiers, Battle of Dien Bien Phu

Resistance efforts managed by resourceful leaders, supported by alliances built carefully over the decades, could topple even the strongest colonial powers and force even the most entrenched foreign occupiers to let go their hold.

HO CHI MINH believed in two things: the Communist revolution and freedom for Vietnam. Neither was imaginable without the other. The Communist ideal was what would give the people the strength to fight. Marxism-Leninism would allow them to come up with winning military strategies. And like-minded countries would supply them with the weapons they needed for victory. In early 1954, as the decisive battle was coming to a head, these were the resources — human, intellectual, and material — that the Vietnamese would have to mobilize. Ho Chi Minh was confident that his people were ready. He looked at how far they'd come since he returned to the country thirteen years earlier. Since he'd taken up quarters in a cave near the Chinese border with a few comrades, including Vo Nguyen Giap, his most faithful disciple. Together they'd created a liberation army, the Viet Minh. Together they'd forged links with the rural population of the area. They'd learned the local language, the local customs, they'd lived exactly the way the people did. And only after they'd done that did they turn to the people's political education. Ho Chi Minh wrote a newspaper and scripted plays. Together they sang, danced, acted. They communicated their ideas.

As their faction grew stronger and more numerous, they started requisitioning the colonists' plantations, those that belonged to the biggest landowners. And redistributing the land to poor farmers. Their popularity shot up, and so did the number of their soldiers. Then in 1949, the Communists won the civil war in China. Vietnam's big neighbor became a powerful ally. Weapons, uniforms, and medicine started to flow into the country. With General Vo Nguyen Giap in command of the Viet Minh and overseeing preparations, the final battle could be allowed to occur.

It would take place at Dien Bien Phu, a basin in northwest Vietnam that the French had decided to turn into a fortress. They'd brought in so many men and so much materiel, they'd devised such a sophisticated defensive strategy, they were certain they would defeat any attack the Vietnamese might mount. The

Local inhabitants ferrying materials into the hills of Dien Bien Phu, Vietnam, in 1954.

CHIẾN DỊCH ĐIỆN BIÊN PHỦ VĨ ĐẠI ĐÃ TOÀN THẮNG!

Viet Minh poster celebrating the victory of Dien Bien Phu.

French were so sure of their readiness that they sent General Giap a message: "What are you waiting for to start the battle?"

A disciplined soldier, Giap was waiting for orders from Ho Chi Minh and the Communist Party Central Committee. The rules of engagement were clear enough: "We do not advance or attack except with the purpose of winning." And to win, Giap would have to do the impossible, right under the noses of the French. He would have to establish himself on all the surrounding mountains. Dismantle the artillery pieces the Chinese had delivered. Haul them up steep and muddy tracks on men's backs. Camouflage them. Bring tons and tons of food along tenuous supply lines for the men who would attack Dien Bien Phu. For three months, 250,000 porters worked day and night. On roads and

trails that the French routinely bombed. Ho Chi Minh's countrymen would do anything for victory. Push modified bicycles carry-
ing five-hundred-pound loads. Bury the dead. Rebuild the roads
after every bombing. Dig trenches, tunnels, and trails into the
sides of hills. In the evenings attend sessions on political education. Never let anyone forget the importance of this gigantic
enterprise.

Although it took place right in front of their eyes, the French
noticed nothing. Because of the constant bombing, they did not
believe for a second that the Viet Minh would manage to put in
place so many troops and so much weaponry. That the mountains around them could be bristling with artillery. That the hills
on which they had established their camps were mined with
galleries.

When General Giap launched the attack on March 13, 1954,
the French realized the Viet Minh had accomplished the impossible. They'd thought they were facing a guerrilla army, but instead
they were confronting battalions of disciplined soldiers who'd
mastered both military maneuvers and trench warfare. After
seven weeks of pitched battle, the French surrendered. Eleven
thousand of their soldiers were taken prisoner. But the Viet Minh
had little use for the rules of war. A forced march of four hundred
miles. Imprisonment under harsh conditions for four months.
Only one prisoner in three would ever make it back to France.

The French had lost, they would have to leave Vietnam. Ho Chi
Minh had won, but he knew the fight was not yet over. Because
the most powerful nation on earth, the United States of America, was at war with Communism. And the United States had no
intention of letting Communist ideology take root in Southeast
Asia. In the meantime, the Vietnamese victory at Dien Bien Phu
gave the lie to the myth of European invincibility. Across the still
colonized world, Dien Bien Phu was hailed as a great feat, and it
filled the hearts of activists with hope. ■

A Decisive Battle:
Turning the Tables on the Colonists

Once the Battle of Dien Bien Phu ended on May 7, 1954, the French tried to transform the grim failure into a glorious defeat, even as anticolonial activists in Asia and Africa celebrated the battle as an astonishing victory. In Algeria a few days later, the news prompted Algerian nationalist militants of the Special Organization, the paramilitary arm of the Movement for the Triumph of Democratic Liberties, to make armed combat a strategic priority. The historian Mohamed Harbi, a former member of the FLN, described Dien Bien Phu as "a sort of payback for the bloody events of May 8, 1945," referring to the massacres at Sétif and Guelma: "The word 'payback' is not exactly adequate, but there was the feeling that someone had finally been able to say: 'Enough!' And Vietnam was in fact a small country, with small means compared to the powerful nation that had occupied it for a century... Vietnam was an important touchstone for other freedom movements."

In 1962 Ferhat Abbas summed up this feeling by calling Dien Bien Phu "the Battle of Valmy of the colonized peoples," referring to the battle that stopped the Prussian invasion of France in its tracks during the French Revolution. We now know that the French defeat at Dien Bien Phu came about partly because a sizable fraction of France's Indigenous troops refused to fight, at a time when they constituted 75 percent of the fighting force. Vietnamese auxiliaries, North African *tirailleurs*, and Thais gathered on the banks of the Nam Youn River and at times clashed with French soldiers. Lieutenant Colonel Bigeard gave the order to open fire on Algerian tirailleurs who were "deserting" the front. The French came to realize the fragility of a colonial system that relied on the cooperation of at least a portion of the "natives." "Let us stop making soldiers who are not of our own race fight for causes that are in fact ours," said Colonel Pierre Langlais, the former commander of the French garrison during the Battle of Dien Bien Phu, in 1962. "The time is past when, through our politics, we can persuade the native population that they are fighting for their own good." On the Vietnamese side, the battle became a founding myth, illustrating the patriotic heroism of the Vietnamese and obscuring significant internal rifts. Much later General Vo Nguyen Giap admitted that during the confrontation with the French he had ordered the suppression of several mutinies, which were judged to be "derelictions of the law."

3. The World Is Ours
(1956–present)

The Antidote

Frantz Fanon boarding a ship, followed by Algerian journalist Rheda Malek

The trauma inflicted by colonial regimes on Indigenous populations was severe, pervasive, and enduring. Yet the forms it took were sometimes subtle and not readily apparent.

SOMETIMES, waiting for his next patient in the heat of the Algerian town of Blida, he would close his eyes and relive a seemingly insignificant memory. In fact this memory was the source and well-spring of his identity and beliefs.

Fort-de-France, Martinique, 1935
His class is on a field trip to visit the monument of Victor Schoelcher. Frantz is ten years old. Like all the kids in this peaceful French colony, he is entitled to this field trip. Schoelcher was the great abolitionist, the patron saint who freed the slaves in 1848. But Frantz doesn't understand why the man is being honored. Why Schoelcher and not the slaves? Why not the men and women who resisted?

Frantz feels that something isn't quite right about this, but he can't put it into words. So he says nothing, and his silence creates a crack, a fissure. A question that will always be with him.

Blida, Algeria, summer 1956
Frantz Fanon is a young psychiatrist. He wants to revolutionize his field. He's chosen to practice in Algeria so he can care for the colonized, those who've been denied the right to be fully human.

That's also why he writes *Black Skin, White Masks*, a clinical study of how to overcome racial alienation. So that Blacks can free themselves of wanting to be white. So that whites can free themselves of the absurd belief in their own superiority.

His patient knocks on the door. Frantz Fanon opens his eyes. As a doctor, he is ready to listen to all sides, whether the patient is Algerian or French. Still, he has trouble with torturers. The man who has just arrived tells him how sore his knuckles get after working a guy over for ten hours straight. He explains to the doctor that he won't put up with even the slightest resistance. To the point where he hit his wife and tied her to a chair because she nagged him about beating their children so often.

Fanon's face shows no emotion. In his head, the police torturer's words clash with those of the victims. For months now, putting his own life at risk, he has been hiding activists in the

Soldiers of Algeria's National Liberation Army undergoing training, July 26, 1967.

Frantz Fanon and fighters of the National Liberation Army in Oujda, Morocco, near the Algerian front.

recesses of the hospital, independence fighters wanted by the French army. Most of them have experienced torture.

To Fanon's way of thinking, the violence imprinted on their minds and bodies sums up the madness of the colonial enterprise. His work in French Algeria no longer makes sense to him. The whole country is sick and needs to be freed. He leaves his position and sets off to join the Algerian FLN.

He embraces not just a people but a revolution, the global uprising of oppressed nations. He makes sense of this rebellion by starting from a simple idea: that what the colonized need to free themselves from first and foremost is the master's gaze. ◼

"We Want to Be Free, Viva l'Algérie!"

In 1958 the soccer player Rachid Mekhloufi, who played for Saint-Étienne, was one of the bright stars of France. He'd been selected for that year's French national team to compete in the World Cup in Sweden. Adored by the French public even while the Algerian War was raging, this young man had left behind the massacres and poverty of his hometown of Sétif and was living the dream. But on April 14, 1958, all that changed. A representative of Algeria's National Liberation Front (FLN) came to recruit him for its team. Overnight, Mekhloufi turned his back on his old life and joined his nation's struggle. With nine other players, he left clandestinely for Tunis, where an apartment was waiting for him along with professional equipment and a better salary than he'd been earning in France.

The new team played for the provisional government of the Republic of Algeria. The FLN backed the team to the hilt, hoping to help raise Algeria's profile on the international scene. France countered by asking FIFA, the sport's governing body, to prohibit its member countries from competing with the Algerian team. Only the Western European countries complied. For four years, Mekhloufi and his teammates measured themselves against teams from Vietnam, China, the Arab world, and Eastern Europe, helping to forge alliances that would benefit Algeria after its independence. At every match, fans chanted in English the slogan that the FLN devised to sway international opinion: "We want to be free, viva l'Algérie!" Thus Algeria's war of independence was fought, at least in part, outside North Africa and the French Empire, in the international arena, on soccer fields, and especially in the field of diplomacy: Algerian nationalists, overpowered militarily, were able to gain a victory by sensitizing many supporters at the United Nations, in the media, and at universities around the world.

After Algeria received its independence in 1962, Mekhloufi for professional reasons went back to playing for the Saint-Étienne club in France. He was afraid of the reception the fans would give him, but the first time he touched the ball the crowd broke into cheers. Mekhloufi ended his playing career by winning the Coupe de France in 1968. The trophy was presented to him by none other than General de Gaulle, president of the French Republic, who said to him somewhat ambiguously: "You are France." But Mekhloufi chose to continue his professional career in Algeria, where he became manager of the new national team, the Fennecs. During a three-to-two victory over France in 1975, the FLN chant was changed to "One, two, three, viva l'Algérie!" And that's still the chant that is heard in the stands today.

The Shooting Star

(L to R) General Cumont of Belgium, President Joseph Kasavubu, and
Prime Minister Patrice Lumumba at Léopoldville's N'Djili Airport, 1960

Gentlemen: The independence of Congo is the end result of the work started with the exceptional personality of King Leopold II, which he tackled with determined courage and which has been continued with persistence by Belgium. It represents a defining moment in the destiny, not only of Congo itself, but I have no hesitation in saying it, of all of Africa.

— KING BAUDOUIN OF BELGIUM

We have witnessed the atrocious sufferings of those who were imprisoned for their political views or their religious beliefs, exiled in their own country, their fate truly worse than death.

Together, my brothers, we will start another fight, a sublime struggle, which will lead our country to peace, prosperity, and greatness.

— PATRICE LUMUMBA

BRUSSELS AIRPORT, APRIL 1956. This trip is one that Patrice Lumumba has been dreaming about for years. It's the ultimate reward. From now on, he'll belong to the Indigenous elite, those that the Belgians call "evolved," the ones they rely on to build the Congo of the future. A Congo where they expect to keep their place, of course.

When you belong to Congo's new ruling elite, you have to show that you're worthy, irreproachable, that your actions will be in keeping with your rank. You have to show the Belgians you deserve their confidence. Lumumba has learned this lesson well. On the first stage of the trip, he has no choice. He takes off his hat before the statue of King Leopold II. The man who, eighty years earlier, had carved out a gigantic territory in the heart of Africa

Patrice Lumumba touring a department store in Brussels during his visit to Belgium in 1956.

and made it into his private property. The man who had built his fortune on the deaths of millions of Congolese men and women.

But Lumumba wants to believe in the future, and the future is full of promise. A political class is coming into existence in Congo, and Lumumba wants to be part of it. He wants to transform his country, turn it into a modern state.

Here in Europe, everything runs smoothly, everything looks sleek. Escalators, functional kitchens, well-behaved children. A vision forms in Lumumba's mind. Tomorrow's Congo will look like this. An ideal country that the "evolved natives" will build hand in hand with the colonizers. A wonderful country where Blacks and whites will be equals.

To get his ideas heard and to break into politics, Lumumba has to raise his profile in Leopoldville, the Congolese capital. Using his networks, he gets a job with a brewery, the Brasserie du Bas-Congo, as director of sales.

His assignment is to capture a major share of the vast "native consumer" market. The word soon gets around that Polar beer flows freely wherever Lumumba goes. His popularity in the capital shoots up. Before long, the drink-fueled evening gatherings turn into political meetings. Lumumba dazzles. Lumumba convinces. Naturally, Lumumba becomes the leader of the newly formed Mouvement National Congolais.

At this point, things are changing at breakneck speed. In 1956, it was taboo even to say the word "independence." Today it's on everybody's lips. Independence. Lumumba wants it more than anything, but he's not in a hurry. True to his earlier ideas, he'd like the transition to go smoothly and with the cooperation of the Belgians.

Lumumba's moderateness is reassuring to the Belgian government, which authorizes Lumumba to attend the first All-African Peoples' Conference in Accra, the capital of Ghana, in December 1958. Big mistake. The conference opens on a note of pacifism. Africa's leaders are all admirers of Gandhi, and they express their belief that the continent will be freed through nonviolence. Then a man walks up to the lectern, a man who believes that, given the colonizer's implacable violence, armed conflict is inevitable. That man is Frantz Fanon, the delegate from Algeria's National Liberation Front.

Faced with French tanks and airplanes, faced with napalm, faced with torture, faced with the destruction of entire villages, do you really think we can counter with passive resistance? If Africa is ever to achieve freedom, it won't be by holding out our begging bowls. We must grab what belongs to us by force. All forms of struggle must be adopted, violence included.

— **FRANTZ FANON**

The room bursts into wild applause. Lumumba is in shock. He's never heard a Black man talk like this. He's never been exposed to such a radical position. But Lumumba strongly believes that the situation in Congo is very different from the situtation in Algeria, that its Belgian colonizers are not as hard-nosed as the French.

Prime Minister Patrice Lumumba and King Baudouin in Leopoldville on June 29, 1960, for the official proclamation of Congo's independence.

After attending the conference in Accra, Lumumba starts to speak more pointedly. The Belgians begin to distrust him. They distrust him, but his popularity is such that they can't stop his rise. Independence is inevitable, and the man associated with it will be Patrice Lumumba. The Belgians had hoped to keep their colony into the 1970s, possibly even into the 1980s. Now, twenty years ahead of schedule, they have to hand over the keys to the country to a man they increasingly view as a traitor. On June 30,

1960, Lumumba becomes the prime minister of the Republic of Congo. On the appointed day, King Baudouin of Belgium arrives in Leopoldville to take part in the independence ceremonies. He climbs to the dais and, with blithe disregard, holds forth on the glories of the colonial venture. He presents independence as the terminus toward which King Leopold's colonizing project had been headed all along.

But Lumumba would not let this final provocation go unanswered. The time had come to stand up and let the voice of the Congolese be heard.

I ask all of you, my friends who tirelessly fought in our ranks, to mark this June 30, 1960, as an illustrious date that will be ever engraved in your hearts, a date whose meaning you will proudly explain to your children, so that they in turn might relate to their grandchildren and great-grandchildren the glorious history of our struggle for freedom.

Independence was won in struggle, a persevering and inspired struggle carried on from day to day, a struggle in which we were undaunted by privation or suffering, and stinted neither strength nor blood. Morning, noon, and night, we endured ironies, insults, and blows because we were Negroes.

We have experienced the atrocious sufferings, being persecuted for political convictions and religious beliefs, and exiled from our native land: our lot was worse than death itself.

Brothers, let us commence together a new struggle, a sublime struggle that will lead our country to peace, prosperity, and greatness.

— PATRICE LUMUMBA

King Baudouin took this speech as an unforgivable affront. It would not go unpunished. But for now, Congo celebrated. Lumumba's words, broadcast live over the radio, electrified the country. ▪

"Africa, Unite!"

Africa unite

Unite for the benefit of your people!

Unite for it's later than you think!

Unite for the benefit of my children!

Africa awaits its creators!

Africa you're my forefather cornerstone!

Unite for the Africans abroad!

Unite for the Africans a yard!

"Africa Unite," the signature song from *Survival*, the 1979 album by Bob Marley and the Wailers, illustrates the revival of pan-Africanism—and music's role in shaping its public expression, a fact noted by W. E. B. Du Bois in *The Souls of Black Folk* (1903). The activists of the 1970s and 1980s took their inspiration from their glorious precursors: Toussaint Louverture, the hero of the Haitian revolution in the late eighteenth century; Menelik II, the emperor of Ethiopia, who dealt the Italian colonizers a decisive defeat at the battle of Adwa in 1896; and the Haitian Benito Sylvain, who took part in the First Pan-African Conference in London in July 1900. The time had come to work toward unifying the Africans scattered among the Americas, Europe, and the African continent.

Itself an experiment in restored unity, the conference marked the founding act of a global Black elite. Its goal was to prove that, whatever the so-called science of race might say, those of African descent could take their fate in their own hands and participate in the progress of humankind. The most telling moment of the gathering was when the bishop of London invited the delegates to tea at the episcopal residence, Fulham Palace. Several of the invitees displayed their musical talents. They were "civilized" Blacks and behaved as any well-brought-up Englishman might. But while this was enough to get them an invitation, it did not get them a hearing. No European leader paid the slightest attention to the demands, modest though they were, formulated in the course of the conference on the subjects of forced labor, segregation, and the "pass" or docket system used for people of color. The question of independence was never even raised, only equality.

Pan-African congresses organized by Black leaders from the United States, the West Indies, and Britain subsequently took place in Paris in February 1919, in Brussels in September 1921, in Lisbon in December 1923, and in New York in August 1927. At the end of World War II, a fifth congress, organized by Kwame Nkrumah of Ghana, was convened in Manchester, England, in October 1945. It marked a turning point in the history of pan-Africanism, which from then on would demand unconditional decolonization. And the congresses that followed all took place in Africa.

Capital of the Revolution

Dave Burrell and Archie Shepp perform at the
1969 Pan-African Cultural Festival in Algiers

The whites were finally leaving. The ones the native populations called the *nassaras*, the *toubabs*, the *mindeles*. In the regions north and south of the Sahara, the independence movements were gradually winning. Africa was becoming itself again. Before long, colonization would be just a bad memory.

ALGIERS, JULY 1969. The country had been independent for seven years. To celebrate, Algerians invited Africans from the four corners of the continent. Africans who had just gained their independence and Africans who were still fighting for it. All of them were getting a chance to see each other in person for the first time.

Something was in the air, a stir of freedom. The participants felt as though a weight had been lifted from their chest. They walked in the streets, breathed the air, danced a little victory jig. *Walla-ye* (in the name of God), it did feel good!

Whether you were Arab, Black, or Berber, you were African. And today was about celebrating. About beauty. About breaking down boundaries — whether between countries or inside people's heads. Africa was being reinvented in black and brown. Above and beyond race. A utopian Africa, a real Africa.

On this day, a new and possible world was being born. A world for all. A world where no one would rule over anyone else. Where each would exist in his or her own right. Where life would wear the face of the other.

This was a moment that you wanted to last forever. A breath of eternity that carried everyone on its wings. ■

Parade through the streets of Algiers to celebrate the opening of the first Pan-African Cultural Festival, July 21, 1969.

Pan-African Cultural Festival in Algiers, celebration at the Caroubier Hippodrome, July 27, 1969.

The New Man Is Zairian!

Kinshasa, October 27, 1971. The streets are flowing with beer, and a rumba rhythm fills the air. Today is officially the day to say goodbye to "Congo" and ring in "Zaire," the country's new name. President Mobutu, who is also the army's chief of staff, made the decree based on his doctrine of *authenticité*. He changed the name of the currency in 1967, and now it's time to change the name of the river and the country. The president himself has been rechristened. Gone is "Joseph-Désiré Mobutu"! A true Bantu, he will be known from now on as "Mobutu Sese Seko Kuku Ngbendu Wa Za Banga," or "Mobutu the warrior who goes from victory to victory and no one can stop him." The self-proclaimed victorious warrior has decided to remake his country in his own image and create an African nation-state on an accelerated schedule, erasing the colonial trauma with a heavy dose of identity therapy. He has ordered all Zairians to give up their Christian names and assume a typically Bantu name. Women are prohibited from wearing skirts in favor of the *kitenge*, and men have to adopt the *abacost*, a Chinese-inspired garment, whose name comes from the French *à bas le costume* (down with the suit).

In 1973–1974, Mobutu nationalized all foreign enterprises (mines, factories, oil prospecting concerns, construction companies), quickly turning them over to members of his family and political supporters. The new owners would drive most of these companies into bankruptcy within a few months, and the businesses were returned to their former owners. To stay in power, Mobutu decided to follow the World Bank's recommendations to the letter, liberalizing the economy and privatizing public services. With its personality cult, its control of private life and personal beliefs, its tortures and executions, the Zaire of the 1970s was a previously untried political experiment: a tropical dictatorship, influenced by China and North Korea but unwaveringly allied to the United States. The politics of Zairization provoked new kinds of resistance—such as SAPE, a group of influencers and tastemakers formed in the 1970s and 1980s to subvert the doctrine of *authenticité* represented by the new national garment, the *abacost*. Following the lead of Adrien Mombele and Papa Wemba, the youth of Kinshasa adopted the dandyish SAPE style and the high-fashion brands of Europe, challenging Mobutu's politicocultural project and single-party government.

The Betrayal

Protest in Paris following the assassination of Patrice Lumumba, 1961

Getting rid of the colonists was one thing. Guiding the ship of state through the turbulence of global politics was another. And the anger that had served the heroes of the decolonizing movement so well, the pride, the burning sense of injustice, were not the same qualities that it took to maintain political power in the fractious postcolonial times. So the leaders of the newly independent nation-states were not always the ones you might expect — or want.

LEOPOLDVILLE, JULY 1960. Congo gained its independence just ten days ago, and already it's threatening to implode. The Belgians, who would go to any lengths to protect the wealth of their old colony, have brought in an army to occupy the country's south. That's where the gold, copper, and uranium mines are located. Without these natural resources, the Congolese nation isn't viable. Patrice Lumumba, the prime minister, calls on the Soviet Union to help him regain control of his territory. With the Cold War at its height, this move provokes the bitter enmity of the United States.

Lumumba counts on the support of the army's new chief of staff, Joseph-Désiré Mobutu, who has always been faithful to him. But it turns out that Mobutu hates the Communists, and he doesn't approve of having the Soviets in his country. Then, too, Mobutu is ambitious, and this looks like a good time to make his move. In great secrecy, the young officer activates his network of contacts in the Belgian and American information agencies. He offers to get rid of Lumumba once and for all.

On December 2, 1960, Patrice Lumumba is arrested. Mobutu exhibits his prisoner as a trophy in front of the world's news cameras. Then he has him killed on the other side of the country.

Patrice Lumumba arrives in Leopoldville on December 2, 1960, after his arrest in Lodi on December 1.

Commemorative ceremony for Patrice Lumumba, staged by President Joseph-Désiré Mobutu on September 9, 1967, in Kinshasa, Democratic Republic of Congo.

So as to leave no trace, Lumumba's body is dissolved in acid. That ends any possibility of a truly independent Congo. It ends Lumumba's dream. Mobutu is now the guarantor of Western interests in central Africa. As long as he controls his country, he can do what he likes. And he intends to rule on his own. Nobody is allowed to oppose him, neither the living nor the dead. But the Congolese people have not forgotten Lumumba — his vision, his destiny, his assassination. Since he can't destroy Lumumba's memory, Mobutu decides to appropriate it.

Patrice Émery Lumumba had the foresight, the firmness, and the courage of a great statesman. He was also an implacable defender of the inalienable rights not just of his own people but of Africa and all mankind. Let it be known therefore that as of June 30, 1966, the Congolese people and its government proclaim Patrice Émery Lumumba a national hero of the Democratic Republic of Congo.

— JOSEPH-DÉSIRÉ MOBUTU

Now that he has washed his hands of the blood of Patrice Lumumba, now that he has rewritten the history of Congo before the eyes of the whole world, he renames himself Mobutu Sese Seko Kuku Ngbendu Wa Za Banga. Translation: "Mobutu the warrior, who goes from victory to victory and whom no one can stop." He is the absolute master of the country, a dictator, and to his friends in the West he is a model for how things should be handled in Africa. With their complicity, he remains in power for thirty-two years. ■

They Dreamed of a Different World

Algiers, which had become the global capital of revolution, hosted the Non-Aligned Movement Summit from September 5 to 9, 1973. The symbolism was powerful. Having won its freedom by military force, Algeria welcomed a multitude of independence movements on its soil, from the African National Congress of South Africa to the Black Panthers of America. It is the advent of the "Third World," a term coined in 1952 by the French scholar Alfred Sauvy to define countries that remained outside either the Western Bloc (NATO) or the Soviet Union

(Warsaw Pact). But Algeria was also looking for international recognition from countries beyond the revolutionary coalition.

For President Houari Boumedienne, who had installed an authoritarian regime in Algeria after his 1965 coup, this called for delicate maneuvering. The Non-Aligned Movement had been founded by Jawaharlal Nehru of India, Marshal Tito of Yugoslavia, and President Sukarno of Indonesia with the aim of supporting independence struggles in Asia and Africa. Most colonies had by this time gained their freedom, but they needed to get their second wind. Their numbers had grown—eighty-three countries participated in the summit—and there were deep divisions among them. The major disagreements concerned what political system to install at home and what alliances to form abroad. Some looked to the West, including President Senghor of Senegal and King Faisal of Saudi Arabia; others, among them Fidel Castro of Cuba, thought that only Moscow could protect them from the heavy hand of America. Muammar Gaddafi of Libya believed that nonaligned countries should reject all foreign alliances. Houari Boumedienne kept the debate from becoming acrimonious by focusing on the question of development.

The Algerian president wanted to establish a new global economic order. He defended the right of peoples to exploit their own riches, on the model of Algeria's nationalization two years earlier of its gas and petroleum industry. But aside from Libya and India, very few countries were in a position to follow such a bold course of action. The nonaligned nations considered creating a fund for the social and economic development of their less fortunate members. The fund would never see the light of day, and solidarity among the countries of the Third World would remain a pipe dream. Nearly forty years later, in May 2014, a thirteenth Non-Aligned Summit was convened in the Palace of Nations in Algiers, to the general indifference of the public. The world had in the meantime become multipolar, and the Non-Aligned Movement had gone out of fashion.

The New World Order

Some former colonies got the statesmen they deserved as leaders. Among the shrewdest was Indira Gandhi, born into India's leading political dynasty. Although she assumed power in India less than twenty years after the country claimed its independence, she soon found herself angling for support from the world's two great superpowers. And with a population of 550 million people, the young nation-state was a force to be reckoned with.

INDIRA HAD NO CHILDHOOD. There wasn't time for that in her family. Only one thing mattered: the struggle to free India. This was a lesson that little Indira Nehru learned even before she could speak. Her grandfather Motilal had founded the Indian National Congress party. Her father, Jawaharlal, led the fight for independence. The famous activist Sarojini Naidu was a family friend. And India's spiritual guide, Mahatma Gandhi, was her godfather. As fate would have it, moreover, she married a man with his last name. It was written in the stars that Indira Gandhi and India were to be one.

On Independence Day her father, Jawaharlal Nehru, became prime minister. For seventeen years, Indira never left his side. Every crisis that occurred during those seventeen years, she navigated with him. Every world figure that he met, she met too. The gilded furnishings, the protocol, the intrigues. Indira watched and learned. When her father died of a heart attack, Indira was ready. She was forty-seven. She quickly rose to lead the country. Indians thought it obvious that the father of the nation should be succeeded by his daughter.

The task that awaited her was gigantic: to lift India out of underdevelopment and make it a twentieth-century power. But

Prime Minister Indira Gandhi of India with President Richard Nixon at the White House, on April 11, 1971.

before she could address the task, she had to deal with the biggest crisis her country had faced since independence. In March 1971, a torrent of men, women, and children streamed across the border separating East Pakistan and India, famished and afraid. They were fleeing death, mass rape, and systematic brutality. Their crime had been to advocate for secession, for the creation of their own country, Bangladesh. They wanted to quit the Pakistani federation. The crisis was one that Indira Gandhi would have to resolve. The Indian prime minister decided to go to Washington and speak to the American president, Richard Nixon, who was the main ally of the Pakistani generals.

It has not been easy to get away at a time when India was beleaguered. To the natural calamities of drought, flood and cyclone has been added a man-made tragedy of vast proportions. I am haunted by the tormented faces in overcrowded refugee camps, reflecting the grim events which have compelled the exodus of millions from East Bengal. I have come here for a deeper understanding of the situation in our part of the world, in search of some wise impulse, which, as history tells us has sometimes worked to save humanity from despair.

— INDIRA GANDHI

During her state visit to the Soviet Union in September 1971, Indira Gandhi met with the secretary general of the Communist Party, Leonid Brezhnev.

Nixon may have smiled for the camera, but he had no intention of shifting his policy. In fact, he continued sending arms to Pakistan. A pragmatist, Indira Gandhi turned to the United States' archenemy, the Soviet Union, with whom she signed a friendship treaty. Knowing that the Soviets now had her back, Gandhi openly signaled her support for the Bangladeshi independence activists. When Pakistan then declared war on India, on December 3, 1971, Gandhi was unperturbed, knowing that her own army was the stronger of the two. The next day she ordered the invasion of East Pakistan. Nixon worried that his Pakistani allies might collapse within a few days. He sent his most powerful nuclear aircraft carrier into the Gulf of Bengal to intimidate Gandhi. But he'd forgotten about the Soviet Union's nuclear submarines. His fleet surrounded, Nixon had to back down.

Pakistan, getting no help from the United States, threw in the towel, and Bangladesh became an independent country. Indira Gandhi had won, thanks to the Soviets, but she didn't want India to be dependent on anyone. She decided that India would develop a nuclear weapon. Less than thirty years after gaining its independence, India joined the select club of nuclear powers. For better or for worse, the former colony was now on an equal footing with the greatest nations on earth. ■

Getting to Food Independence

When Jawaharlal Nehru died suddenly in 1964, India was at a crossroads. Seventeen years had passed since India achieved independence, but though the country's industrial infrastructure was starting to fall into place, the threat of famine recurred year after year. The partition of India had removed vast tracts of fertile land from India's territory and put them across the border in Pakistan. To make up for a structural shortage of grain, India was importing wheat from the United States. The country urgently needed a way to feed its population, and the Indian National Congress, if it wanted to stay in power, had to honor its independence promises. Its leaders unexpectedly found an ally in the United States.

With the Cold War at its height, the United States was anxious to contain the spread of Communism in Asia. Its diplomacy borrowed from the thinking of the Rockefeller Foundation, which had for the past twenty years been acting on the premise that the best way to fight creeping Soviet influence was to mount an attack on world hunger. Those who suffered from famine clearly offered a prime target for Communist propaganda, and Washington's solution was to provide food. In Mexico, the Rockefeller Foundation had developed varieties of wheat that gave excellent yields, as long as they were dosed with sufficient amounts of pesticides and chemical fertilizer. The new high-yield wheat seed was delivered to India and Pakistan in 1965, as the two countries went to war with each other for the second time in their history. But the conflict would last less than three weeks, and the seed proved to fulfill all expectations on both sides of the border. Both states would be able to feed their populations and add a fresh page to their national saga, in which the "Green Revolution" would play an important part. Today, South Asia is having to face the many environmental consequences of this sudden development of intensive agriculture, based as it is on the massive application of polluting fertilizers and on heavy irrigation, which increases the soil's salinity and depletes groundwater.

The Battle of Southall

Protest against the killing of Blair Peach, Southall, 1979

To a family of recent immigrants, the new country is often cold and impassive. But the parents arrive with their religion, their culture, the glorious history of their ancestors fresh in their minds. And they are eager to transmit this cultural heritage to their children in all its vivid detail. The children, meanwhile, are trying to absorb the new culture they're immersed in. And just as often rejected by.

IMAGINE you're from an immigrant family. Twenty-five years ago, your parents emigrated to England in the hope of finding a better life. They bust their chops day after day so you can have a future. They work in factories, in kitchens. In the belowground floors of the subway, in the mud of construction sites. Uncomplainingly, they build the country of their former colonists. They just want you to go to school, fly right. Be successful. Not really a whole lot to ask. Only what any parent hopes for. And you don't want to shatter their dreams. So you don't tell them that you've been getting beaten up from the first day by children who've been taught to hate the color of your skin. You grit your teeth and take it. But the older you get, the more the violence escalates. These racist kids invent a new sport, they call it Paki-bashing. They don't care whether your parents come from India, Pakistan, or Bangladesh. Whatever. To them you're a Paki, an inferior creature, a victim.

One day in 1976, Gurdip Singh Chaggar, an eighteen-year-old Sikh, is stabbed by a bunch of young whites in Southall, a peaceful town west of London. That day, everything changes. That day, the brown-skinned youths decide to take their fate into their own hands. It's time for them to stop listening to their parents, who beg them not to antagonize the English. It's time to stand up for the right to be British like everyone else. When the far right

British policemen block protesters marching in opposition to the National Front in Southall, London, on May 24, 1979.

National Front Party decides to hold a meeting at the town hall, the young people of Southall are ready and waiting for them.

More than 2,800 policemen flood the streets to protect a hand-

ful of militant racists. Tensions escalate, and the order goes out for the crowd to disperse.

Some of the protesters take shelter in a space belonging to Misty in Roots, a local reggae band. The police enter, lash out at anything that moves, and crack the skull of the band manager,

Protesters against the National Front in Southall, Curtain Road, London, on August 20, 1978.

Clarence Baker. He is in a coma for five months. A few hundred yards away, Blair Peach, an activist with the Anti-Nazi League, tries to flee. No luck. A policeman bludgeons him with a night-stick. Unable to speak and with his eyes rolled upward, Blair Peach is transported to the hospital. He dies four hours later. The whole town gathers for his funeral service. Indians, Blacks, and whites fought side by side against the National Front. Together, they've taken back control of their neighborhoods. The victory, though painful, is complete. The far right militants don't dare set foot in Southall again. The Ruts, a punk band from Southall, will take the events of that day, April 24, 1979, and make them into an epic song, "Jah War." It's a hit, and they perform it on concert stages across Europe, a hymn for a cosmopolitan generation that dreams of finally shaking off the demons of racism and colonization. ∎

Respect: The Talbot Automotive Strike (1982–1983)

In June 1982 French television viewers learned that the working class in France had undergone a color shift. Two automotive factories in the Paris region, the Peugeot plant in Aulnay-sous-Bois and the Talbot plant in Poissy, had gone on strike, and most of the striking workers were immigrants from former French colonies in North Africa and the Sahel. To the classic demands for higher pay and better work conditions they added a demand for dignity, the freedom to unionize, and equality. The strikers hoped that the new labor-friendly leftist government would help their cause. The strike was a success, and in the aftermath thousands of immigrant workers joined France's major labor organizations, the CGT and the CFDT.

There followed a period of constant ferment at Citroën, Peugeot, and Talbot, though these car makers had not previously experienced any strikes for decades. The immigrants were subject to the authority and hazing of the in-house unions, which often had ties to the far right. The many Moroccan workers had an additional threat hanging over them: if they enrolled in the CGT, the organization reported them to the Moroccan consulate in Paris, and they risked being arrested by the police on their next visit back to their native country. But even this threat didn't discourage the workers, and strike after strike was called. The political power wielded by postcolonial immigrants worried the ownership class as well as the French government, which looked for ways to hobble this new social movement. An economic downturn soon gave them the opportunity. The auto industry went through a rough patch, and in 1983 Talbot announced a plan to lay off two thousand workers. Despite a CGT strike in December, the plan went ahead. Virtually all the laid-off workers were North Africans, sub-Saharans, or West Indians. In early January, the strikers clashed with members of the in-house union, the Confédération des Syndicats Libres, who were affiliated with extremist militants of the far right Parti des Forces Nouvelles. Their slogans included: "Arabs in the ovens, Blacks in the Seine." The strike failed, but for the first time immigrants from France's former colonies were spearheading a major social movement in the home country. Part of the left tried to deligitimize the movement's political claims, however, by raising the specter of Islamism. France's minister of the interior, Gaston Deferre, speaking on national radio, characterized the strikes at the Renault plant bluntly: "This is the work of Shiite fundamentalists."

Once Upon a Time in Nollywood

Filming of Nigerian director Kunle Afolayan's *October 1*

Africans, even from a country that has securely achieved its independence, are apt to feel they start off at a disadvantage. That they're playing in the minor leagues. The world looks down on their whole continent, despises it, a residue of the long years of colonialism. But Africans found a weapon at hand, one of the most powerful in the modern arsenal—the movies. And they have been quick to put it to good use.

LAGOS, 1992. Day after day, Okechukwu Ogunjiofor walks the city's streets, through the din of traffic and the stench of tailpipe exhaust. He sells pens, handkerchiefs, beauty products. He imagined a different life for himself. He dreamed of becoming a filmmaker, a crazy dream for the son of a teacher, but he managed to attend the national television school. When he graduated, though, all his hopes collapsed. The International Monetary Fund had just put Nigeria under surveillance. From one day to the next, the government had to reduce its expenses. The television industry stopped hiring. Movies were no longer subsidized. The upshot was that no one in the country was making films.

Okechukwu could pack up his dreams of becoming a filmmaker. Like thousands of other unemployed degree holders, he became a street peddler.

Yet Okechukwu was convinced that the country needed Nigerian films. That homegrown films were essential. People sat in their houses and watched movies from China, the United States, India, everywhere except Africa. And a revolution in image production was occurring. The Japanese had just invented the video recorder, which put live-action images within everyone's reach. Okechukwu jumped on it. He would make movies directly onto video cassette, bypassing film altogether. Adding up all the costs,

Publicity poster for the film *Ibu & Adaku in London*, 2015.

The song "Gbona" by Burna Boy received more than 36 million views on YouTube, contributing to the global success of Nollywood, which produces advertisements and music videos as well as films.

he figured he would need one thousand dollars. He talked a businessman into backing his crazy project. He would make the cheapest movie in the history of film.

To cut back on costs even further, Okechukwu played one of the main roles himself. He wrapped the movie in two weeks. It's known as *Living in Bondage*. Immediate success. Hundreds of thousands of copies were sold throughout the country. Despite being pirated, *Living in Bondage* earned its producer $140,000. One hundred forty times its initial investment, a bonanza! Okechukwu Ogunjiofor had hit on a miraculous recipe — to tell universal stories about love, betrayal, and money, but anchored in Nigerian reality and using the local languages.

The success of *Living in Bondage* prompted the emulation of a whole generation. A new movie industry was born. It was known as "Nollywood," the Nigerian Hollywood.

In less than twenty years, Nollywood would become the third largest movie center in the world, after America and India. The industry invented itself as it went along, building on its successes and making movies in every genre from romantic comedy to fantasy, to action. In Lagos and the surrounding area, where Okechukwu Ogunjiofor first had the idea in 1992 to shoot a movie on video, a million people now work in the audiovisual industry. A million Africans who are exporting their Afro-futurist vision across the world. ■

Decolonizing Thought

And what if the West were to squarely face its history of colonial rule, recognizing how central colonialism has been to its essential nature? And what if we were to try to analyze how, in constructing its representation of the Other, the West shored up its power and forged its identity? These basic questions inspired a book that, in 1978, detonated like a bomb in the intellectual world: *Orientalism*, by Edward Said, a professor at Columbia University in New York. Of Palestinian descent, Said analyzes a number of literary, scholarly, and graphic works in the European canon, from Goethe to Conrad, and including Flaubert and Delacroix.

In Said's telling, these authors have created a fictional Orient, monolithic and timeless. Their Orient is feminine, barbaric, degenerate, despotic, and illogical, the opposite of Europe, which is civilized, virile, and rational. This supposed difference in nature between the West and the Orient provides a justification for Europe's domination of the rest of the world. More broadly, this set of images lies at the very foundation of the modernist tendency in the contemporary West.

During the decades from 1980 to 2000, Edward Said's thesis spurred further research into colonialism, which could no longer be considered exclusively the business of the colonized countries. The fact of colonization also strongly marked the nations that were once colonial powers. New research has highlighted the cultural dimensions of colonial rule. However, it has tended at times to objectify the West, just as the European Orientalists of the nineteenth century objectified the Orient. The colonizers, according to their national and social origins, generated a variety of utterances that can at times be contradictory.

Furthermore, Edward Said managed to overlook an important player—the colonized themselves, who are too often considered passive victims. This view obscures the process of negotiation between colonists and the Indigenous elites and the resistance strategies deployed by the colonized peoples, not to mention their complete indifference to the fact of colonization. Indigenous elites and informants have often played a crucial role in the shaping of colonial studies, tailoring them to provide a base for their own social and political power. But since the 1980s, the field of postcolonial studies has been deeply enriched by the South Asian scholars of the Subaltern Studies Group, who have promoted a "history from below" designed to restore the voices of the "voiceless" and those who are "absent" from history—which is to say most colonized people.

The Last Battle

Veteran Mau Mau fighter Ngugi Munyoike at the inauguration
of the war memorial at Uhuru Park, Nairobi, 2015

The legacy of colonialism survives it. The empires are empires no longer, the colonies are independent states, but the colonial past still walks abroad. It inhabits the material conditions of today's world. And it lives in the minds of the elders, the trajectory of whose lives was broken by the colonizers, often their bodies as well. This was the case in Kenya, for example, where the British crushed the Mau Mau revolt in the 1950s. But the elders' voice has not been silenced, nor has their thirst for justice. What follows is testimony that forced an admission of responsibility from the British government, a tentative first step in exorcizing the demon.

THE WHITES left fifty years ago. But for the last of the Mau Mau, it's as though it was yesterday. Because what the English took away from them can never be returned. Their womanhood, their manhood, their honor. Because some wounds never heal. Today the survivors are ready to talk about it.

Luvai came toward me with pliers, he took hold of my testicles. And he squashed them with the pliers. I almost died.

— PAULO MUOKA NZILI

My hands were tied behind my head, I was blindfolded, my legs were tied. They stuck a bottle in my vagina. I've had no pregnancy since. The bottle destroyed my uterus.

— NAOMI NZIULA

They ordered us to lie on the ground, one on top of the other. There were five of us at least. They came around between our legs to do nasty things. Then they whipped us several times. They did unspeakable things to us.

— JANE MUTHONI MARA

At a protest on September 12, 2015, a veteran of the Mau Mau wars holds up a photograph of Jomo Kenyatta's arrest in October 1952. Kenyatta would later become president of independent Kenya.

They forced a man to put his head into a bucket of water. Then the white officer raised one of the man's legs, and the guard grabbed the other. Another guard brought sand and pushed it into the prisoner's anus with a stick. I'd never seen anything like that. I didn't think it was possible. I still have nightmares about it to this day. It was something that should never happen to a human being.

— PASCASIO MACHARIA

The former Mau Mau combatants never lost their energy for the fight. They organized again, patiently. They methodically gathered six thousand witness statements. Now they wanted to bring the British government to trial.

Yet even if thousands of them told the same story, the words of the old Mau Maus would not be enough. To convict the former colonial power, you would need proof — transcripts, private notes, and direct orders conclusively establishing, decades after the fact, that atrocities were committed, that they were part of a deliberate system, that they were sanctioned at the highest levels. To find these documents, the former Mau Mau needed allies. They needed historians, lawyers, former colonial administrators. Whites who would line up on their side. Britons who believed the trial was crucial, a unique opportunity to bring the truth to light. The colonial administrators had planned to destroy all the evidence systematically before the advent of independence. So that they could leave with their heads held high, with every memory and trace of their atrocities erased. But in fact the work was poorly done. Some archivists, more conscientious than the rest, saved a portion of the documents, which show that Her Majesty's government ordered the acts of torture.

Esther Miano, 82, a former Mau Mau fighter, cries out for justice in Nairobi, Kenya, on September 12, 2015.

When, after years of litigation, the Mau Maus' lawyers managed to obtain these documents, the British government knew it had lost. Rather than engage in a risky lawsuit, rather than allow months of revelations about the horrors committed fifty years earlier in the name of colonization, the British authorities decided to negotiate. With their back to the wall. On June 6, 2013, the minister of foreign affairs, William Hague, admitted (though with a thousand caveats and circumlocutions) that, Yes, Great Britain took responsibility for the tortures and murders in Kenya. Accepted its colonial heritage. Assumed moral responsibility for its acts, finally.

The British government recognizes that Kenyans were subjected to torture and other forms of ill treatment at the hands of the colonial administration. The British government sincerely regrets that these abuses took place, and that they marred Kenya's progress toward independence.

— WILLIAM HAGUE

The Mau Maus' victory was huge. They forced the former colonial power to face up to the crimes committed in Britain's name — the horror of those crimes, their absolute evil. They forced England to abandon its moral superiority. More importantly, they forced it to admit the existence of the Other. In accomplishing this unprecedented act, a small group of elderly Kenyans made the point that history could not be written without them. This narrative now belongs to all of us. Whoever our ancestors, whatever they did, and whatever was done to them. ▪

The Empire Strikes Back

The time when the British Empire imposed its will on the rest of the world is long gone. At this point, the United Kingdom almost deserves our commiseration, given how deep a crisis Brexit has brought about. The nation's exit from the European Community was backed by British conservative politicians nostalgic for the colonial era. They apparently believe Great Britain will naturally reassume its global role once its ties to the former territories of the Commonwealth have been renewed. Consequently, on her first state visit outside Europe, in November 2016, Prime Minister Theresa May traveled to India, which she described as "our most important and closest friend." High on her list of priorities was to meet with the directors of the Tata Group, an Indian multinational conglomerate preparing at that time to lay off four thousand workers from its steel mill in Wales. The British prime minister appeared determined to prevent this at all costs.

The executives of the Indian company, however, categorically refused to meet with her. Ironically, this mirrors an event that occurred 140 years earlier when the British colonial administrators refused to give Jamsetji Tata, founder of the industrial dynasty, the right to build a steel mill of his own, as the British wanted to keep their monopoly on steel production. Today, the economic leverage has changed hands. The Tata Group is not only a giant in the metal industry on the Indian subcontinent, it has bought the Corus steelmaking group in Britain. Also Jaguar, Land Rover, and Tetley, the tea company! Tata is therefore deeply entwined with British identity and pride, key elements of which are held by entrepreneurs in Mumbai. And this has happened at a time when the former colony is becoming richer than the former home country: in 2019, India became the fifth-ranked world power, surpassing the United Kingdom. This offers a hint of historical revenge for India, which was the second-ranked world power in the eighteenth century, before English rule.

On the subcontinent today, this spectacular shift is represented by the Hindu ultranationalist Narendra Modi. A man of his time, Modi applies his aggressive nationalist politics, which are in line with those of Vladimir Putin, Donald Trump, and Xi Jinping, both domestically and internationally. And his politics are perfectly adapted to a "cool" hypermodernity. The Indian city of Bangalore, closely connected with Silicon Valley, is a major player in globalization. As are the chief executives at Google, Microsoft, and MasterCard, who are all members of the Indian diaspora. These men and women, multilingual and cosmopolitan, are a product of India's colonial history. But they now govern empires without borders, where domination is independent of color and country. Of course, Indian's victory and sweet revenge on its ex-colonizers is unique. Algeria, Morocco, Senegal, Kenya, Nigeria, and more are still lagging behind. However, the balance of power and influence has shifted toward Asia, and with Africa's population weighted toward a young and promising generation, it's entirely possible that this continent will be next in showing the way to the rest of the world.

Bibliography

General Works

Arendt, Hannah. *Imperialism: Part Two of The Origins of Totalitarianism*. New York: Houghton Mifflin, 1951.

Brocheux, Pierre, ed. *Les Décolonisations au XXᵉ siècle*. Paris: Armand Colin, 2012.

Burbank, Jane, and Frederick Cooper. *Empires in World History: Power and the Politics of Difference*. Princeton, NJ: Princeton University Press, 2010.

Cooper, Frederick. *Africa in the World: Capitalism, Empire, Nation-State*. Cambridge, MA: Harvard University Press, 2014.

Cooper, Frederick. *Citizenship between Empire and Nation: Remaking France and French Africa, 1945–1960*. Princeton, NJ: Princeton University Press, 2014.

Cooper, Frederick. *Colonialism in Question: Theory, Knowledge, History*. Berkeley: University of California Press, 2005.

Darwin, John. *Britain and Decolonization: Retreat from Empire in the Post-War World*. London: Macmillan, 1988.

Duara, Prasenjit. *Decolonization: Perspectives from Now and Then*. London: Routledge, 2004.

Klein, Jean-François, Pierre Singaravélou, and Marie-Albane de Suremain. *Atlas des empires coloniaux (XIXᵉ au XXᵉ siècles)*. Paris: Autrement, 2012.

Singaravélou, Pierre. *Les Empires coloniaux XIXᵉ–XXᵉ siècle*. Paris: Seuil, 2013.

Singaravélou, Pierre, and Sylvain Venayre, eds. *Histoire du monde au XIXᵉ siècle*. Paris: Fayard, 2017.

1. Apprenticeship

THE HEROIC PRINCESS

Deshpande, Prachi. "The Making of an Indian Nationalist Archive: Lakshmibai, Jhansi, and 1857." *Journal of Asian Studies* 67, no. 3 (August 2008): 855–79.

Joshi, P. M. "1857 and the Rani of Jhansi." *Bulletin of the Deccan College Post-graduate and Research Institute* 29, no. 1–4 (1968–1969): 153–64.

Singh, Harleen. *The Rani of Jhansi: Gender, History, and Fable in India.* Delhi: Cambridge University Press, 2014.

THE HEIST OF THE CENTURY

Brunschwig, Henri. "La négociation du traité Makoko." *Cahiers d'études africaines* 5, no. 17 (1965): 5–56.

Chamberlain, Muriel E. *The Scramble for Africa.* London: Longman, 1974.

Savorgnan de Brazza, Pierre. *Conférences et lettres de P. Savorgnan de Brazza sur les trois explorations dans l'Ouest africain de 1875 à 1886. Texte publié et coordonné par Napoléon Ney.* Paris: Dreyfous, 1887.

Stanley, Henry Morton. *The Congo and the Founding of Its Free State: A Story of Work and Exploration.* London, 1885.

Surun, Isabelle. "Conférence de Berlin, 1884–1885." In *Histoire du monde au XIXe siècle*, edited by Pierre Singaravélou and Sylvain Venayre. Paris: Fayard, 2017.

FILLING SKULLS

Blanckaert, Claude. *De la race à l'évolution. Paul Broca et l'anthropologie française, 1850–1900.* Paris: L'Harmattan, 2009.

Firmin, Anténor. *The Equality of the Human Races: Positivist Anthropology.* Translated by Asselin Charles. New York: Garland, 2000.

Fluehr-Lobban, Carolyn. "Anténor Firmin: Haitian Pioneer of Anthropology." *American Anthropologist* 102, no. 3 (September 2000): 449–66.

Singaravélou, Pierre. *Professer l'empire. Les "sciences coloniales" en France sous la IIIe République.* Paris: Publications de la Sorbonne, 2011.

Conrad, Joseph. *Heart of Darkness*. London, 1899.

Hochschild, Adam. *King Leopold's Ghost: A Story of Greed, Terror, and Heroism in Colonial Africa*. New York: Houghton Mifflin Harcourt, 1998.

Lindqvist, Sven. *"Exterminate All the Brutes": One Man's Journey into the Heart of Darkness and the Heart of European Genocide*. Translated by Joan Tate. New York: New Press, 1997.

Mussai, Renée, and Mark Sealy, curators. *Congo Dialogues: Alice Seeley Harris and Sammy Baloji*. An exhibition shown at Autograph, Rivington Place, London, January 14 to March 7, 2014. https://autograph .org.uk/exhibitions/congo-dialogues.

Ndaywel è Nziem, Isidore. *Nouvelle histoire du Congo. Des origines à la République démocratique*. Brussels: Le Cri; Kinshasa: Buku Édition, 2014.

Stengers, Jean. *Le Congo. Mythes et réalités, cent ans d'histoire*. Gembloux, Belgium: Duculot, 1989.

Thompson, Jack T. "Light on the Dark Continent: The Photography of Alice Seeley Harris and the Congo Atrocities of the Early Twentieth Century." *International Bulletin of Missionary Research* 26, no. 4 (2002): 146–49.

Twain, Mark. *King Leopold's Soliloquy*. Boston: Warren, 1905.

MOHUN BAGAN'S REVENGE

Bandyopradhyay, Kausik. *Scoring off the Field: Football Culture in Bengal, 1911–1980*. New Delhi: Routledge India, 2011.

Majumdar, Boria. "The Vernacular in Sports History." *Economic and Political Weekly* 37, no. 29 (July 2002): 3069–75.

Singaravélou, Pierre, and Julien Sorez, eds. *L'Empire des sports. Une histoire de la mondialisation culturelle*. Paris: Belin, 2010.

WORLD WAR I: THE BLACK FORCE

Mangin, Charles. *La Force noire*. Paris: Hachette, 1911.

Michel, Marc. *Les Africains et la Grande Guerre. L'appel à l'Afrique (1914–1918)*. Paris: Karthala, 2003.

Murphy, David. "Tirailleur, facteur, anticolonialiste: la courte vie militaire de Lamine Senghor (1924–1927)." *Cahiers d'histoire. Revue d'histoire critique* 126 (2015): 55–72.

Sagna, Olivier. "Lamine Senghor (1889–1927), un patriote sénégalais engagé dans la lutte anticoloniale et anticapitaliste." Master's thesis, directed by Catherine Coquery-Vidrovitch, University of Paris 7, 1980–1981.

Sarr, Amadou Lamine. *Lamine Senghor (1889–1927). Das Andere des senegalesischen Nationalismus.* Vienna: Böhlau, 2011.

A WOMAN INSURGENT

Ekechi, Felix K. "Perceiving Women as Catalysts." *Africa Today* 43, no. 3 (July–September 1996): 235–49.

Oduol, Wilhelmina A. "Kenyan Women in Politics: An Analysis of Past and Present Trends." *Transafrican Journal of History* 22 (1993): 166–81.

Thuku, Harry. *An Autobiography.* Nairobi: Oxford University Press, 1971.

Wipper, Audrey. "Kikuyu Women and the Harry Thuku Disturbances: Some Uniformities of Female Militancy." *Africa: Journal of the International African Institute* 59, no. 3 (1989): 300–37.

THE PARIAH'S CONSCIENCE

Birchall, Ian. "*Le Paria.* Le Parti communiste français, les travailleurs immigrés, et l'anti-impérialisme (1920–1924)." *Contretemps. Revue de critique communiste* (March 2011).

Boittin, Jennifer A. *Colonial Metropolis: The Urban Grounds of Anti-imperialism and Feminism in Interwar Paris.* Lincoln: University of Nebraska Press, 2010.

Dewitte, Philippe. *Les Mouvements nègres en France, 1919–1939.* Paris: L'Harmattan, 1985.

Goebel, Michael. *Anti-imperial Metropolis: Interwar Paris and the Seeds of Third World Nationalism.* Cambridge: Cambridge University Press, 2015.

McKay, Claude. *Banjo: A Story without a Plot.* New York: Harper and Brothers, 1929.

Senghor, Lamine. *The Rape of a Country.* In *White War, Black Soldiers: Two African Accounts of World War I.* Edited by George Robb. Translated by Nancy Erber and William Peniston. Indianapolis: Hackett, 2021.

Courcelle-Labrousse, Vincent, and Nicolas Marmié. *La Guerre du Rif: Maroc, 1921–1926*. Paris: Seuil, 2009.

Daoud, Zakya. *Abdelkrim, une épopée d'or et de sang*. Paris: Séguier, 1999.

El Moudden, Abderrahmane. "Réforme par le bas: aux origines de la guerre populaire, la guerre de résistance de Muhammad Ben Abd al-Karim (1920–1926)." *Oriente moderno* 23, no. 84 (2004): 165–74.

Roger-Mathieu, J., ed. *Mémoires d'Abd-el-Krim*. Paris: Librairie des Champs-Élysées, 1927.

2. Liberation

THE INDIGENOUS INTERNATIONALE

Dugrand, Alain, and Frédéric Laurent. *Willi Münzenberg: Artiste en révolution (1889–1940)*. Paris: Fayard, 2008.

Dullin, Sabine, and Brigitte Studer. "Communisme + transnational. L'équation retrouvée de l'internationalisme au premier *XX*^e^ siècle." *Monde(s)* 10, "Communisme transnational" special feature (2016): 9–32.

Hargreaves, John D. "The Comintern and Anti-colonialism: New Research Opportunities." *African Affairs* 92, no. 367 (April 1993): 255–61.

Petersson, Fredrik. "La Ligue anti-impérialiste: un espace transnational restreint, 1927–1937." *Monde(s)* 10, "Communisme transnational" special feature (2016): 129–50.

Senghor, Lamine. *The Rape of a Country* in Bakary Diallo, *White War, Black Soldiers: Two African Accounts of World War I*. Cambridge: Hackett, 2021.

THE STRONGER SEX

Alexander, Meena. "Sarojini Naidu: Romanticism and Resistance." *Economic and Political Weekly* 20, no. 43 (October 26, 1985): WS68–71.

Chatterjee, Manini. "1930: Turning Point in the Participation of Women in the Freedom Struggle." *Social Scientist* 29, no. 7–8 (July–August 2001): 39–47.

Gandhi, Mahatma. *The Mahatma and the Poetess: Being a Selection of Letters Exchanged between Gandhiji and Sarojini Naidu*. Compiled by

E. S. Reddy. Edited by Mrinalini Sarabhai. Mumbai: Bharatiya Vidya Bhavan, 1998.

Naravane, Viswanath S. *Sarojini Naidu: An Introduction to Her Life, Work and Poetry.* Hyderabad: Orient BlackSwan, 1996.

Norvell, Lyn. "Gandhi and the Indian Women's Movement." *British Library Journal* 23, no. 1 (spring 1997): 127.

FROM HONG KONG WITH LOVE

Brocheux, Pierre. *Ho Chi Minh: A Biography.* Translated by Claire Duiker. Cambridge: Cambridge University Press, 2007.

Brocheux, Pierre, and Daniel Hémery. *Indochina: An Ambiguous Colonization, 1858–1954.* Translated by Ly Lan Dill-Klein, with Eric Jennings, Nora Taylor, and Noémi Tousignant. Berkeley: University of California Press, 2009.

Duncanson, Dennis J. "Ho Chi Minh in Hong Kong, 1931–1932." *China Quarterly* 57 (January–March 1974): 84–100.

THE BATTLE OVER CASTE

Gehlot, N. S. "Dr. Ambedkar, Mahatma Gandhi and Dalit Movement." *Indian Journal of Political Science* 54, no. 3–4 (July–December 1993): 382–87.

Jaffrelot, Christophe. *Dr. Ambedkar, leader intouchable et père de la Constitution indienne.* Paris: Presses du Science Po, 2000.

Tiwari, Shailender Kumar. "Social Justice: Gandhi and Ambedkar." *Indian Journal of Political Science* 70, no. 2 (April–June 2009): 429–39.

Verma, Vidhu. "Colonialism and Liberation: Ambedkar's Quest for Distributive Justice." *Economic and Political Weekly* 34, no. 39 (September 25–October 1, 1999): 2804–10.

DETERMINED TO WRITE

Ageron, Charles-Robert. "Mai 1945 en Algérie: enjeu de mémoire et d'histoire." *Matériaux pour l'histoire de notre temps* 4, no. 108 (2012).

Bouchène, Abderrahmane, Jean-Pierre Peyroulou, Ouanasa Siari Tengour, and Sylvie Thénault, eds. *Histoire de l'Algérie à la période coloniale, 1830–1962.* Paris: La Découverte, 2012.

Déjeux, Jean. "Les structures de l'imaginaire dans l'œuvre de Kateb Yacine." *Revue des mondes musulmans et de la Méditerranée* (1973): 267–92.

Peyroulou, Pierre. *Guelma, 1945*. Paris: La Découverte, 2009.

Vautier, René. *Déjà le sang de mai ensemençait novembre*. A documentary film. UPCB (Union de production cinématographique bretonne), 1982.

Yacine, Kateb. *Nedjma*. Translated by Richard Howard. Charlottesville: University Press of Virginia, 1991.

BREAKING AWAY

Gilmartin, David. "The Historiography of India's Partition: Between Civilization and Modernity." *Journal of Asian Studies* 74, no. 1 (2015): 23–41.

Khan, Yasmin. *The Great Partition: The Making of India and Pakistan*. New Haven: Yale University Press, 2007.

Markovits, Claude, ed. *A History of Modern India, 1480–1950*. Translated by Nisha George and Maggie Hendry. London: Anthem Press, 2004.

Weber, Jacques. "La question du Cachemire et les relations indopakistanaises: de la partition à la guerre de 1965." *Guerres mondiales et conflits contemporains* 195 (September 1999): 9–33.

WAMBUI'S OATH

Cleary, A. S. "The Myth of Mau Mau in Its International Context." *African Affairs* 89, no. 35 (April 1990): 227–45.

Elkins, Caroline. *Britain's Gulag: The Brutal End of Empire in Kenya*. London: Pimlico, 2005.

Elkins, Caroline. *Imperial Reckoning: The Untold Story of Britain's Gulag in Kenya*. New York: Henry Holt, 2010.

Howarth, Anthony, and David Koff, producers. *The Black Man's Land Trilogy: Colonialism, Nationalism and Revolution in Africa*. A documentary film. United States: Anthony David Productions, 1973.

Meriwether, James H. "African Americans and the Mau Mau Rebellion: Militancy, Violence, and the Struggle for Freedom." *Journal of American Ethnic History* 17, no. 4 (summer 1998): 63–86.

Otieno, Wambui Waiyaki. *Mau Mau's Daughter: A Life History*. Boulder, CO: Westview Press, 1992.

Brocheux, Pierre, and Daniel Hémery. *Indochina: An Ambiguous Colonization, 1858–1954*. Translated by Ly Lan Dill-Klein, with Eric Jennings, Nora Taylor, and Noémi Tousignant. Berkeley: University of California Press, 2009.

Journoud, Pierre. *Diên Biên Phu. La fin d'un monde*. Paris: Vendémiaire, 2019.

Journoud, Pierre. "Diên Biên Phu: naissance et destin d'un mythe héroique." In *Héros militaire, culture et société (XIXᵉ–XXᵉ siècles)*. Villeneuve-d'Ascq: Publications de l'Institut de recherches historiques du Septentrion, 2012.

Vo, Nguyen Giap. *Dien Bien Phu, Rendez-Vous with History: A Memoir*. Translated by Lady Borton. Hanoi: The Gioi, 2004.

3. The World Is Ours

THE ANTIDOTE

Cherki, Alice. *Frantz Fanon: A Portrait*. Translated by Nadia Benabid. Ithaca, NY: Cornell University Press, 2006.

Connelly, Matthew. *L'Arme secrète du FLN. Comment de Gaulle a perdu la guerre d'Algérie*. Collection "Petite Bibliothèque Payot." Paris: Payot, 2014.

Fanon, Frantz. *Alienation and Freedom*. Edited and compiled by Jean Khalfa and Robert J. C. Young. Translated by Robert Corcoran. London: Bloomsbury Academic, 2018.

Fanon, Frantz. *Œuvres*. Paris: La Découverte, 2011.

Macey, David. *Frantz Fanon: A Biography*. New York: Picador Press, 2000.

Rochebrune, Renaud de, and Benjamin Stora. *La Guerre d'Algérie vue par les Algériens*. Paris: Denoël, 2019.

THE SHOOTING STAR

Boukari-Yabara, Amzat. *Africa Unite! Une histoire du panafricanisme*. Paris: La Découverte, 2014.

Etambala, Zana Aziza. "Lumumba en Belgique, du 25 avril au 23 mai 1956: son récit de voyage et ses impressions. Document inédit." In *Figures et paradoxes de l'Histoire au Burundi, au Congo et au Rwanda*, edited by Marc Quaghebeur. Brussels: L'Harmattan, 2002.

Omasombo, Jean, and Benoît Verhaegen. *Patrice Lumumba, acteur politique. De la prison aux portes du pouvoir (juillet 1956—février 1960)*. Paris: L'Harmattan, 2005.

CAPITAL OF THE REVOLUTION

Hare, Nathan. "A Report of the Pan-African Festival." *Black Scholar* 1, no. 1 (November 1969): 2—10.

Khellas, Mériem. *Le Premier Festival culturel panafricain, Alger, 1969: une grande messe populaire*. Paris: L'Harmattan, 2014.

Mazzoleni, Florent. "Les musiques des indépendances africaines." *Africultures* 1, no. 83 (2011).

Mokhtefi, Elaine. *Algiers, Third World Capital: Freedom Fighters, Revolutionaries, Black Panthers*. London: Verso, 2018.

THE BETRAYAL

Dugrand, Camille. "Politique de la rumba congolaise. Une musique entre subversion et révérence." *Revue du Crieur* 5 (2016): 52—61.

Langellier, Jean-Pierre. *Mobutu*. Paris: Perrin, 2017.

Michel, Thierry, director. *Mobutu, King of Zaire*. A documentary film. Brussels: Les Films de la Passerelle, Image Création, Les Films d'Ici, Radio Télévision Belge Francophone, and Canal +, 1999.

Tshonda, Jean Omasombo. "Lumumba, drame sans fin et deuil inachevé de la colonization." *Cahiers d'études africaines* 44, no. 173—74 (2004): 221—61.

Weissman, Stephen R. "What Really Happened in Congo: The CIA, the Murder of Lumumba, and the Rise of Mobutu." *Foreign Affairs* 93 (2014): 14—24.

THE NEW WORLD ORDER

Gupte, Pranay. *Mother India: A Political Biography of Indira Gandhi*. New York: Scribner's, 1992.

Jaffrelot, Christophe, ed. *L'Inde contemporaine de 1950 à nos jours*. Paris: Fayard, 1996.

Jayakar, Pupul. *Indira Gandhi: A Biography*. New York: Pantheon Books, 1992.

Malhotra, Inder. *Indira Gandhi: A Personal and Political Biography*. Boston: Northeastern University Press, 1991.

Roy, Arundhati. *The Cost of Living*. New York: Modern Library, 1999.

THE BATTLE OF SOUTHALL

Baumann, Gerd. *Contesting Culture: Discourses of Identity in Multi-ethnic London*. Cambridge: Cambridge University Press, 1996.

Gilroy, Paul. "Police and Thieves." In *The Empire Strikes Back: Race and Racism in 70s Britain*. London: Routledge, 2004.

Young Rebels: The Story of the Southall Youth Movement. Audiovisual, digital, and print materials. Developed by The Asian Health Agency, in partnership with Digital:Works. London: Bishopsgate Institute, 2014.

ONCE UPON A TIME IN NOLLYWOOD

Akinola, Olabanji. "The Rebirth of a Nation: Nollywood and the Remaking of Modern Nigeria." *Global South* 7, no. 1 (spring 2013): 11–29.

Alabi, Adetayo. "Introduction: Nollywood and the Global South." *Global South* 7, no. 1 (spring 2013): 1–10.

McCain, Carmen. "Nollywood and Its Others: Questioning English Language Hegemony in Nollywood Studies." *Global South* 7, no. 1 (spring 2013): 30–54.

Onuzulike, Uchenna. "Nollywood: The Birth of Nollywood: The Nigerian Movie Industry." *Black Camera* 22, no. 1 (spring–summer 2007): 25–26.

THE LAST BATTLE

Elkins, Caroline. *Imperial Reckoning: The Untold Story of Britain's Gulag in Kenya*. New York: Henry Holt, 2010.

Engelhart, Katie. "Rule Britannia: Empire on Trial." *World Policy Journal* 29, no. 4 (winter 2012–2013): 94–105.

Kenya: White Terror. A documentary film. https://www.youtube.com/watch?v=XVoudfKrzTQ BBC, 2002.

Wahome, Ephraim, Felix Kiruthu, and Susan Mwangi. "Tracing a Forgotten Heritage: The Place of Mau Mau Memory and Culture in Kenya." In *Conservation of Natural and Cultural Heritage in Kenya: A Cross-disciplinary Approach*, edited by Anne-Marie Deisser and Mugwima Njuguna, 212–26. London: UCL Press, 2016.

Quotation Sources

PREFACE

"To brush history against the grain": Walter Benjamin, "Theses on the Philosophy of History," 1940 essay reprinted in *Illuminations: Essays and Reflections*, trans. Harry Zohn, edited and with an introduction by Hannah Arendt (NY: Schocken Books, 1969): 256–57.

"Until the lions have their own historians": Chinua Achebe, interview with the *Paris Review* 133, Winter 1994.

ALICE IN LEOPOLD LAND

Alice Seeley Harris: cited from interview with BBC, 1970. Diary extract in Judy Pollard Smith, *Don't Call Me Lady: The Journey of Alice Seeley Harris* (Bloomington, IN: Abbott Press, 2014).

"Within the German borders": Von Trotha, cited in Dr. Ewelina U. Ochab, "The Herero-Nama Genocide: The Story of a Recognized Crime, Apologies Issued and Silence Ever Since," *Forbes*, May 24, 2018.

THE BLACK FORCE

"Africa cost us mountains of gold": Adolphe Messimy

"not spare Black blood": General Nivelle

A WOMAN INSURGENT

"Take my dress": Mary Nyanjiru cited in Valentine Udoh James and James S. Etim, eds., *The Feminization of Development Processes in Africa: Current and Future Perspectives* (Westport, CT: Praeger, 1999).

THE PARIAH'S CONSCIENCE

"France recognizes us": Lamine Senghor, quoted in Jean-Blasé Kololo, "Lamine Senghor: 'La Défense de la race nègre,'" *Cahiers Léon Trotsky* 73 (March 2001), 76.

"to assist all freedom movements": French Communist Party

"Intellectuals of various Eastern nationalities": India House manifesto, 1909.

"university of international encounters": Armando Bazán

PUBLIC ENEMY NUMBER ONE

"From every point on earth": Lamine Senghor, *Le Paria*.

"Is there some racial or national prejudice": Abd el-Krim, letter to European powers, summer 1922.

"Flying over the Rif mountains": Ernesto "Che" Guevara, June 14, 1959.

"The strategy followed by Abd el-Krim": *Chicago Tribune*.

THE INDIGENOUS INTERNATIONALE

"The imperialist oppression": Lamine Senghor entry in *Le Maitron*, http://maitron-en-ligne.univ-paris1.fr/spip.php?article 130989.

"Since Senghor's arrival": Agent L. Josselme, September 22, 1926, in ANOM (Archives nationales d'outre-mer) Slotfom 3, carton 24.

THE STRONGER SEX

"Friends, I come to you": Interview, October 26, 1928, New York, Fox Movietone archives.

"The body of Gandhi": Sarojini Naidu, quoted in Manini Chatterjee, "1930: Turning Point in the Participation of Women in the Freedom Struggle," *Social Scientist* 29, no. 7–8 (July–August 2001): 39–47.

"The [present] government has no power": M. K. Gandhi, *Young India: 1919–1922* (New York: B. W. Huebsch, 1923), 482–83; M. K. Gandhi, *Voice of Truth* (Ahemadabad: Navajivan Publishing House, 1969), 43.

FROM HONG KONG WITH LOVE

"The path to Paris and London": Leon Trotsky, letter dated August 5, 1919, RAGASPI f, 325, op. I, d. 47, l. 1–2.

"I'm taking advantage": Nguyen Ai Quoc cited in Daniel Hémery, *Hô Chi Minh. De l'Indochine au Vietnam* (Paris: Gallimard, 1990), 145.

"Backward Europe and Progressive Asia": Vladimir Lenin, *Pravda*, 31 May 1913.

THE BATTLE OVER CASTE

"Unfortunately, I was born an untouchable": Bhimrao Ramji Ambedkar, speech given October 13, 1935, in Yeola, cited in *Selected Speeches of Dr. B. R. Ambedkar (1927–1956)*, ed. by D. C. Ahir (New Delhi: Blumoon Books, 1997).

DETERMINED TO WRITE

"The war was over" and "The army occupied the village": Kateb Yacine, interview in the documentary *Déjà le sang de Mai ensemençait Novembre*, by René Vautier, 1982.

BREAKING AWAY

"The time has come": Sarojini Naidu, "My Father, Do Not Rest," broadcast on *All India Radio*, February 1, 1948.

WAMBUI'S OATH

"The Mau Mau": Malcom X, *Malcom X Speaks: Selected Speeches and Statements*, ed. George Breitman (New York: Grove Weidenfeld, 1990). Also https//www.youtube.com/watch?v=Roodpsp2_r8.
"terrorist group": Malcolm Johnson, *The Defender*.
"buy their wives": Malcolm Johnson, *Atlanta Daily World*.
"We support African political aspirations": J. C. Satterthwaite cited in P. Godfrey Okoth, "U.S. Foreign Policy toward Kenya, 1952–1960," 39.

THE ANTIDOTE

"You are France." https://en.wikipedia.org/wiki/Rachid_Mekhloufi.

THE SHOOTING STAR

"Gentlemen: The independence of Congo": King Baudouin of Belgium, from https://en.m.wikisource.org/wiki/Congolese_Independence_speech _by_King_Baudouin_on_June_30,_1960.
"We have experienced": Patrice Lumumba
"Brothers, let us commence together": Patrice Lumumba

"Faced with French tanks and airplanes": Frantz Fanon, "Pour nous employons la violence," *Œuvres* (Paris: La Découverte, 2011), 413–18.

"I ask you all of you, my friends": Patrice Lumumba, SONUMA archive, June 30, 1960.

THE BETRAYAL

"Patrice Émery Lumumba": Joseph-Désiré Mobutu, June 30, 1966, cited in Thierry Michel, *Mobutu, roi du Zaïre* (Brussels: Les Films de la Passerelle, Image Création, Les Films d'Ici, Radio Télévision Belge Francophone, and Canal +, 1999).

"Third World": Alfred Sauvy

THE NEW WORLD ORDER

"It has not been easy": Indira Gandhi, quoted in *M. V. Kamath: A Journalist at Large*, compiled by Kalindi Randeri (Mumbai: Jaico Publishing House, 2006), 95.

THE BATTLE OF SOUTHALL

"This is the work of Shiite fundamentalists": Gaston Deferre

ONCE UPON A TIME IN NOLLYWOOD

"history from below": Subaltern Studies Group

THE LAST BATTLE

Paulo Muoka Nzili, Naomi Nziula, Jane Muthoni Mara: cited from *Kenya's Mau Mau: The Last Battle* (Al Jazeera UK, 2013).

Pascasio Macharia: cited from *Kenya: White Terror* (BBC, 2002).

William Hague: William Hague, minister of foreign affairs, Chamber of Commons, London, June 6, 2013. https://www.gov.uk/government/news/statement-to-parliament-on-settlement-of-mau-mau-claims.

Theresa May: cited in "India Is Britain's 'Most Important and Closest' Friend: Theresa May," *Times of India*, November 6, 2016.

Playlist

Episode 1

Asian Dub Foundation, "Assassin"

Kanika Kapoor, featuring Dr. Zeus, "Jugni Ji"

Wandel Momo Sounah, "Felenko Yéfé"

Leyla McCalla, "Mesi Bondye"

Moisi, Magdalena & Teresa, "Lyo-o-o"

Franco, "Kinsiona"

Mulamba Pania Kapota, "La vida del un negro"

Panjabi MC, "Mundian To Bach Ke"

Zao, "Ancien combattant"

The Famous Nyahururu Boys, "Mwendwa"

Leyla McCalla, "Peze Café"

Oum, "Nia"

Episode 2

Fadoul, "Maktoub Lah"

Geoffrey Oryema, "Ye Ye Ye"

The Skatalites, "James Bond"

JB Lenoir, "Vietnam Blues"

Phuong Dung, "Dô Ai"

Lili Boniche, "Bambino"

Ayub Ogada, "Kothbiro"

Lê Thu, "Sao Biên"

Robert Wagner, "Ride of the Valkyries"

Hùng Cuòng, "Mot Tram phan tram Em Oi"

Episode 3

Niska, featuring MHD, "Versus"

Leyla McCalla, "Kamèn sa w fè"

Souad Massi, "Raoui"

Meryl, "Béni"

Maravillas du Mali, "Lumumba"

E. T. Mensah and the Tempos, "Ghana Freedom"

Fela Anikulapo Kuti, "Colonial Mentality"

Nitin Sawhney, "Homelands"

Swami Baracus, "Stand Strong (Ode to Blair Peach)"

The Ruts, "Jah War"

Burna Boy, "Gbona"

Ayub Ogada, "Dala"

Kalambya Boys, "Kivelenge"

Special Thanks

Marie-Hélène Barberis

Nathalie Beaux

Vincent Bollenot

Vladimir Cagnolari

Juliana Carneiro de Moraes

Fabrice Coat

Marie Corberand

Delphine Coulin

Erwan Denis

Jacques Denis

Christine Doublet

Ève Feuilloy

Bastien Gens

Jeremy Harding

Samuel Hirsch

Leela Jacinto

Mira Kamdar

Reda Kateb

Véronique Lagoarde-Ségot

Claire Le Cam

Geoffrey Le Guilcher

Christine Marier

Olivier Marquezy

Margot Mendès France

Ahmed Baba Miské

Annick Miské-Talbot

David Murphy

Ilana Navaro

Isabelle Paillet

Simon Pannetrat

Mélissa Petitjean

Song Pham

Adam Shatz

Karina Si Ahmed

Sonia Rolley

Chafik Sayari

Johann Zarca

Ranwa Stephan

Rym Debbarh-Mounir

Djan, Elsa, Iris, Juliette, Lily, Lisa, Milena

International Scientific Committee

Frédéric Cooper

Mamadou Diouf

Richard Drayton

Caroline Elkins

Eric Jennings

Philippa Levine

Achille Mbembe

Nguyen Thi Hanh

Valérie Piette

Radhika Singha

Image Credits